Welcome to the February 200... Presents!

This month read the final installment of Lynne Graham's trilogy VIRGIN BRIDES, ARROGANT HUSBANDS, *The Spanish Billionaire's Pregnant Wife*. Leandro Marquez ruthlessly stops at nothing to wed Molly when he discovers she's pregnant with his child! And don't miss the first part of our fabulous new series INTERNATIONAL BILLIONAIRES, which starts when shy, hardworking Holly is swept off her feet by the magnificent Prince Casper in Sarah Morgan's *The Prince's Waitress Wife*. Expect emotions to reach fever pitch in Carole Mortimer's *The Mediterranean Millionaire's Reluctant Mistress* when tycoon Alejandro is determined to claim his secret baby and possess Brynne in the process. And will an innocent plain Jane convince Sheikh Tair Al Sharif to let go of his mistrustful nature in Kim Lawrence's *Desert Prince, Defiant Virgin?* Business tycoon Santos Cordero is intent on seducing Alexa into a marriage of convenience in Kate Walker's *Cordero's Forced Bride,* while sexual tension heightens when Stefano seeks revenge after being left at the altar in Kate Hewitt's *The Italian's Bought Bride.* Be prepared for a battle of the sexes in Robyn Grady's *Confessions of a Millionaire's Mistress* as Celeste and Ben find they want the same thing in the bedroom…but different things from life! Plus, look out for Nicola Marsh's *The Boss's Bedroom Agenda,* in which a sizzling night spent together between Beth and her gorgeous new boss, Aidan, changes everything!

We'd love to hear what you think about Harlequin Presents. E-mail us at Presents@hmb.co.uk, or join in the discussions at www.iheartpresents.com and www.sensationalromance.blogspot.com, where you'll also find more information about books and authors!

Carole Mortimer
THE MEDITERRANEAN MILLIONAIRE'S RELUCTANT MISTRESS

HARLEQUIN®

TORONTO • NEW YORK • LONDON
AMSTERDAM • PARIS • SYDNEY • HAMBURG
STOCKHOLM • ATHENS • TOKYO • MILAN • MADRID
PRAGUE • WARSAW • BUDAPEST • AUCKLAND

Recycling programs
for this product may
not exist in your area.

ISBN-13: 978-0-373-12797-9
ISBN-10:   0-373-12797-9

THE MEDITERRANEAN MILLIONAIRE'S RELUCTANT MISTRESS

First North American Publication 2009.

www.eHarlequin.com

Printed in U.S.A.

All about the author...
Carole Mortimer

CAROLE MORTIMER is one of Harlequin's most popular and prolific authors. Since her first novel was published in 1979, this British writer has shown no signs of slowing her pace. In fact, she has published more than 135 novels to date!

Her strong, traditional romances, with their distinct style, brilliantly developed characters and romantic plot twists, have earned her an enthusiastic audience worldwide.

Carole was born in a village in England that she claims was so small that "if you blinked as you drove through it you could miss seeing it completely!" She adds that her parents still live in the house where she first came into the world, and her two brothers live very close by.

Carole's early ambition to become a nurse came to an abrupt end after only one year of training, due to a weakness in her back suffered after a fall. Instead, she went on to work in the computer department of a well-known stationery company.

During her time there, Carole made her first attempt at writing a novel for Harlequin. "The manuscript was far too short and the plotline not up to standard, so I naturally received a rejection slip," she says. "Not taking rejection well, I went off in a sulk for two years before deciding to have another go." Her second manuscript was accepted, beginning a long and fruitful career. She says she has "enjoyed every moment of it!"

Carole lives "in a most beautiful part of Britain" with her husband and children.

"I really do enjoy my writing, and have every intention of continuing to do so for another twenty years!"

For Peter

CHAPTER ONE

'MR SYMMONDS, would you kindly inform your client that her behaviour when I went to collect Miguel from her home yesterday was unreasonable—'

'Mr Shaw, would you kindly inform your client that I consider his behaviour yesterday worse than unreasonable—it was positively inhuman!' Brynne's eyes sparkled deeply blue and her cheeks flushed with temper as she glared across the room at the man who stood so tall and broodingly remote in front of the window of his lawyer's office. Alejandro Santiago's swarthily attractive face was half in shadow as he returned her gaze.

Paul Symmonds, her own lawyer, spoke reasonably as he sat beside her. 'I'm afraid, Miss Sullivan, that Señor Santiago really does have the law on his side—'

'Perhaps he does—'

'There is no "perhaps" about it, Miss Sullivan. The judge decreed three weeks ago that, as I am Miguel's father, his place is now with me,' Alejandro informed her glacially. 'But when I called at your home yesterday, as was prearranged, you refused to hand Miguel over to me.'

'Michael is a six-year-old boy,' she said, deliberately using the English version of her nephew's name, 'who recently lost the only parents he has ever known in a car crash. He is not some parcel left at the lost-luggage department for you, as his natural father, to just collect and move on!' She was breathing hard in her agitation, and her hands were clenched at her sides.

What she really wanted to do was scream and shout, to tell this man that, although it might have been proved he was Michael's natural father, and she was only his aunt by marriage, the little boy was staying with her.

Except she knew that wasn't going to happen. The legal battle with this man was already over, a private legal battle—a battle Brynne had lost—that had nevertheless received much publicity in the press.

But she wanted to shout anyway.

Alejandro eyed her coldly, his harsh good looks, from his Spanish heritage, completely unemotional.

He was tall, with slightly long dark hair and the coldest grey eyes Brynne had ever seen, his face was all hard angles, and the tailored business suit he wore added to his air of cool detachment. He was a man Brynne had come to dislike as well as fear over the last few weeks as she fiercely opposed his claim on Michael.

'I am well aware of Miguel's age, Miss Sullivan,' he rasped stiffly in response to Brynne's outburst. 'I am also aware, as I am sure are you, that, as my son, his place is now with me,' he added with determination.

'He doesn't even know you!' she protested.

'I am aware of that too,' the tall Spaniard dismissed abruptly. 'Unfortunately there is nothing I can do about the six years of my son's life that have been lost to me—'

'You could have tried marrying his mother seven years ago!' Brynne scorned.

Alejandro's nostrils flared angrily. 'You have no idea of the circumstances! Do not presume to tell me what I could or could not have done seven years ago!' he amended harshly.

'Damn it.' Brynne choked, deciding to tell him what he should have done more recently instead. 'For the last three weeks, since the judgement was ruled in your favour, I've been waiting in vain for you to use that time to get to know Michael. But you haven't even attempted to see him. In fact, I'm not even sure you've still been in the same country!'

His hard grey gaze narrowed icily. 'Where I have been for the last three weeks is none of your—' He broke off impatiently, turning to the two watching and listening lawyers. 'Mr Symmonds, can you not explain to your client that she has no legal right to keep my son from me? The only reason I agreed to this meeting today in the presence of our respective lawyers was as a courtesy to her—'

'So that you didn't have to go back into court, you mean.' Brynne sneered in disgust.

'I do not fear meeting you again in a court of law, Miss Sullivan,' Alejandro Santiago assured her coolly. 'We both know that you would lose. Again.' His mouth twisted. 'But I accept that you are fond of the boy—'

'Fond of him?' she echoed, outraged. 'I love him. Michael is my nephew—'

'He is not, in fact, related to you by blood at all,' the Spaniard told her harshly. 'Miguel was already four years old when his mother married your brother—'

'His name is Michael!' she bit out tautly.

'Look, Miss Sullivan,' Paul Symmonds cut in smoothly. 'I did advise you before this meeting today that you really have no choice but to—'

'Michael is still deeply distraught by the loss of his parents,' Brynne continued to protest, still upset herself at the death of her older brother and his wife in the car crash that had left Michael orphaned. 'I'm sure, when he made his ruling, that the judge believed Mr Santiago would use this three-week interim period to get to know Michael, not that he would just—just suddenly turn up on my doorstep and expect to take Michael away with him!'

Alejandro raised his dark brows, impatiently wondering why this woman continued to fight him. She had done so now for the last six weeks since it had been revealed that her nephew, through her brother's marriage to the boy's mother, was actually Alejandro's son from a brief relationship he'd had with Joanna seven years ago.

If Brynne Sullivan thought that revelation had left him unmoved then she was mistaken, he thought grimly.

It had been awful to read in the newspapers of the horrific motorway crash that had killed eight people, including Joanna and her husband, Tom.

But the photograph in the newspaper of Joanna's son, the little boy who had miraculously survived the collision, and who bore a startling likeness to Alejandro at that age, had been enough to arouse his suspicions as to the boy's paternity.

He had followed up these suspicions with discreet enquiries about Joanna and Michael, quickly learning that the little boy had been four years old when Joanna had married Tom Sullivan, and that there had never been a father in evidence before that time.

That information had certainly shown that the timing and circumstances seemed right, and together with the child's clear likeness to himself there was a clear possibility that Miguel could be his son.

Alejandro had flown to England immediately in order to make further enquiries, and then eventually make his legal claim, a claim that had resulted in the judge ordering tests to be taken in order to prove or disprove his paternity.

It had been proved beyond doubt!

But this woman, this Brynne Sullivan, the younger sister of Joanna's husband, still continued to fight that decision.

By calling him inhuman amongst other things!

He stepped away from the window impatiently. 'As I have said, this meeting today was a courtesy only, and now it is over.'

'No, it isn't,' Brynne protested firmly.

'Yes, it most assuredly is,' Alejandro insisted in measured tones, very near to the end of his patience with this infuriating woman. 'You will have Miguel's things packed and ready so that he can leave with me by this time tomorrow—'

'No, I won't.' Brynne gave a firm shake of her head. 'I can't let you just take him like this—'

'I'm afraid you have no choice in the matter, Miss Sullivan,' Alejandro's lawyer interjected gently. 'The law really is on Señor Santiago's side.'

He received a glittering blue glare for his trouble as Brynne turned to look at him.

Under different circumstances Alejandro would have thought the woman attractive, with her slender figure, long titian-coloured hair, creamy complexion, sparkling blue eyes and air of youthful confidence. But as the only thing that stood between him and his newly recognized son, he instead found her irritating in the extreme!

'Then the law is an ass!' she bit out angrily in answer to the lawyer's remark.

Under different circumstances, Alejandro would also have found her stubborn determination amusing as he recognized in her a will as indomitable as his own.

But the circumstances were not different, and as such Brynne Sullivan was just an irritant he wanted removed. As soon as possible!

His lawyer looked at her pityingly. 'Whether it's an ass or not, Miss Sullivan, Señor Santiago's claim of paternity has been proven and upheld.'

'He doesn't love Michael as we do!' Brynne said as she glared at Alejandro with undisguised dislike. 'Michael was only four when Joanna and Tom married, and now that they're dead my parents and I are the only family he has left—'

'He has grandparents, an uncle and aunt, and two cousins, in Spain,' Alejandro interrupted derisively.

'He doesn't know them any more than he knows you!' she retorted tartly.

He drew in a deep, controlling breath. 'Miss Sullivan, you have made the same argument for the last six weeks,' he cut in impatiently. 'But as I have already stated, neither you nor your parents are related to Miguel by blood—'

'You really are a monster, aren't you?' Brynne

stood up to accuse heatedly. 'Michael still has night-mares because his mother and the only father he has ever known are now dead. How can you even think about wrenching him away from the people he believes to be his grandparents and his aunt in this callous way?'

'I am merely taking what is mine,' Alejandro ground out coldly, still unsure of how he felt towards Joanna for keeping his son's existence from him all these years.

Admittedly their own relationship had been of short duration, nothing more than a holiday affair, but that didn't alter the fact that Joanna had to have known Miguel was his son, and had chosen not to tell him.

Brynne glared at him in frustration. She knew that it had been medically proven that Michael was this man's natural son. She also knew that legally he now had the right to take Michael wherever he wanted.

She had never really stood a chance of keeping Michael, not once Alejandro Santiago proved his claim as the little boy's father. How could a single woman of twenty-five, a schoolteacher, possibly compete with a man who counted his money in millions of pounds, owned homes all over the world and flew around the world on business in his own private jet? The simple answer was, she couldn't. But that hadn't stopped her from trying!

'I really do not have any more time to waste on this subject,' the arrogant Spaniard turned to tell the lawyers sharply. 'I have business commitments in Majorca that I have already neglected the last twenty-four hours—'

'Heaven forbid ensuring Michael's future happiness

should interrupt your work schedule!' Brynne snapped scathingly.

Cold grey eyes raked over her dismissively before Alejandro turned back to Paul Symmonds. 'Now would be a good time for you to once again advise your client to have Miguel ready to leave for Majorca with me when I call for him at her apartment at ten o'clock tomorrow morning,' he stated briskly. 'Anything else will result in my bringing further legal action against Miss Sullivan,' he added grimly.

He would do it too, Brynne acknowledged in defeat as she looked at the implacability of the man's expression.

It still seemed incredible to her that her beautiful, fun-loving sister-in-law, Joanna, could ever have been involved with a man like Alejandro Santiago. Aged in his mid-thirties, he was just too arrogantly self-assured. Too cold. Too—too immediate, she acknowledged, although she recognized that his height, overlong dark hair and arrogantly chiselled features made him the epitome of tall, dark and handsome.

A fact Brynne, despite her anger and frustration with his claim on Michael, had been all too aware of herself the last six weeks.

Had he been as emotionally aloof seven years ago? Or had something happened during that time to make him this way…?

Not that it mattered; the courts had decided to uphold his rights as Michael's father, and there wasn't a damn thing Brynne could do about it.

She looked challengingly at Alejandro. 'Haven't you forgotten something, Mr Santiago?'

Alejandro's eyebrows raised. 'Have I?'

'Oh, yes,' Brynne Sullivan informed him triumphantly. 'The judge made several other rulings, one of them being that it would be best for Michael to stay with me for a further three weeks so that he could complete the summer school term.'

He eyed her warily. 'Which is now over…'

'But he also ruled that, as my school year is now over for the summer too, that if I wished to do so, I might be allowed to accompany Michael for the first month of his stay with you. In order to ensure Michael's—smooth transition into his new life,' she said, unable to disguise the disgust in her voice.

Alejandro was aware the judge had made that compromise to what was obviously a delicate situation. It just wasn't one that he had ever thought this woman, disliking him as she so obviously did, would ever take up!

Brynne Sullivan, he was sure, would be nothing but a nuisance if she came to Majorca with him and Miguel, and would no doubt disagree with him over every decision he made concerning his son's future.

'That would seem to be the ideal solution to Michael's immediate comfort, don't you think, Señor Santiago?' Paul Symmonds prompted carefully while Alejandro looked at his own lawyer with a frown and received only an acquiescent shrug in reply.

What of his own comfort? Alejandro inwardly fumed. He didn't doubt that if he agreed to this the rebellious Brynne Sullivan would enjoy making life difficult for him for the next four weeks.

Brynne wasn't any happier at the prospect of going to Majorca than Alejandro looked at the idea of taking her there. For one thing she was all too aware of the fact that, despite everything, she actually found the man attractive, nerve-tinglingly so.

But practically she knew her presence would be of help to Michael in learning to accept his change of circumstances. It wouldn't make parting from him at the end of that month any easier for Brynne, but at least she could try and ensure that Michael was reconciled to living with his new father.

She had tried to explain things to Michael, of course, but as a six-year-old he really hadn't been able to understand the complexities of the situation.

'Mr Santiago…' She looked across at him confrontationally, well aware that the wariness she felt towards him was more than reciprocated.

Not surprisingly, really; she had fought this man every inch of the way the last six weeks. A battle Brynne had been destined to lose.

But accepting this man's legal right to his son, and then just walking away while he took Michael from all the people who loved him, were two distinctly different things!

Alejandro gave a dismissive shrug of those broad shoulders. 'It is of little interest to me whether or not you choose to accompany Miguel to Majorca, Miss Sullivan,' he snapped dismissively.

'I'm sure that it isn't,' she replied irritably, her face flushed with resentment.

'But if that is your decision then I advise that you also be ready to leave with Miguel tomorrow morning at ten,' he concluded harshly.

So cold. So intransigent. So damned arrogant!

Only the thought of being with Michael for another

month could ever have persuaded Brynne to spend even another second in the company of this man she should have disliked intensely, but who instead made her legs feel slightly weak just looking at him, and her pulse race!

CHAPTER TWO

'DID you see the swimming pool, Aunty Bry? And the beach as we drove up here? Aunty Bry, did you see the beach?' Michael asked excitedly as he slid open one of the two glass doors that led onto the terrace of the bedroom that Alejandro had informed him was to be his for the duration of their stay here. Alejandro had then stiffly informed Brynne that she could use the bedroom next door. 'I can see the beach from here, Alej—er, Father,' Michael corrected awkwardly as he spoke to the tall, silent man who had accompanied them up the stairs. 'The sea is all bluey-green. And the sand is almost white. And—'

'Don't get too close to the rail, Michael,' Brynne instructed instinctively as she followed him outside, glad of a few seconds' respite from Alejandro's overpowering presence.

The warmth of the late July Majorcan sun instantly beat down on her as she looked at the one-hundred-and-eighty-degree view of the tiered orange groves leading down to the ocean.

It wasn't difficult to understand Michael's enthrallment at his new surroundings. If the two of them had just been here on holiday together then Brynne would have been thrilled by the view and location of Alejandro's villa too, but knowing she would be going alone when she left here in a month's time certainly took the edge off any excitement she might have felt at their luxuriously opulent surroundings.

She should have known that the Spaniard's Majorcan home would be like this.

After being on the private jet that had flown them here, with its twelve seats that were actually like armchairs, and a young man who had supplied them with a lunch that any exclusive London restaurant would have been proud to serve, Brynne didn't think anything was going to surprise her ever again!

This magnificent hillside villa was unbelievable though, she thought. Surrounded by terraces on every level, the marbled interior was wonderfully cool after the hour-long drive from the airport, the white furnishings adding to that feeling of coolness, and the swimming pool was glittering invitingly as an alternative to the tempting beach and cool Mediterranean Sea.

Despite his initial feelings of apprehension Michael had become absolutely captivated with his new surroundings as soon as they had got on the private jet earlier this morning. If he had continued to be a little shy of his new darkly brooding father, who once aboard the jet had ignored them both completely as he had become engrossed in some papers he had taken from his briefcase, then it hadn't been enough to dampen the little boy's enthusiasm once they had been airborne.

Brynne wished she could share his youthful pleasure,

but, unlike Michael, she had been totally aware of Alejandro Santiago's presence for the whole of the flight, and then again as he had sat with them in the back of the limousine that had been waiting to drive them from the airport along the west coast of the island to this incredible villa.

No longer wearing one of the formal suits that were all Brynne had seen him in during their legal battle, he looked tall, overpowering and ruggedly handsome in black tailored trousers and a black short-sleeved shirt that was obviously more suitable attire for the warmer climate they were flying to.

Alejandro's manner had been formally polite when he had arrived at her apartment earlier this morning, and he hadn't shown any sign of emotion when he had seen that Brynne was packed and ready to accompany Michael, after all.

In fact, he hadn't acknowledged her presence at all, she thought. Any remarks he had made had been addressed to 'Miguel'—remarks Michael had completely ignored until he had realized he was the 'Miguel' being referred to!

Seeing the two of them together like this made Brynne achingly aware of exactly why Alejandro had been so sure Michael was his son. Both were dark-haired and grey-eyed, and even Michael's baby face was starting to show some of the harder angles of his father's features. The fact that Michael was also tall for his age indicated that he would probably eventually attain his father's considerable height too.

'I do not believe I have ever given you cause to think that I will be—a strict father to Miguel,' Alejandro said tersely as he saw Brynne's tearful gaze rest indulgently on Miguel as he ran from one side of the terrace to the other in order to look at the amazing views over the valley and sparkling blue sea.

She turned to look at him, her eyes appearing bluer and larger than ever, with tears balanced precariously on the edge of her long, dark lashes. 'So far you haven't given me reason to think you will be any sort of father to him!' she replied tartly.

Perhaps because he still found it difficult to believe he was Miguel's father!

Not that he questioned it for a moment; he knew from the medical tests that there could be no doubt. But it had been a very short journey from having suspicions on seeing Miguel's photograph in the newspapers to having them confirmed so positively. A journey that had been dogged by Brynne's stubborn refusal to relinquish Miguel to his custody.

His mouth tightened. 'I have asked that drinks be served on the terrace beside the pool when you have freshened yourself from the journey.' Turning to open the bedroom door, he called, 'Miguel?'

Like ordering a puppy to heel, Brynne thought resentfully as Michael scampered happily out of the room with the man who was now his father. As expected, her own presence here did seem to be making it much easier for the little boy to accept his change of circumstances.

She sat down heavily on Michael's bed, momentarily burying her face in her hands as the tears that had threatened earlier now fell hotly down her pale cheeks.

Tears that had been long overdue.

Too shocked after the car accident that had killed

Joanna and Tom to do more than try to keep herself emotionally together for her grieving parents and the stunned Michael, Brynne hadn't had the opportunity to release her own grief. But now, in the middle of all the luxury that Alejandro Santiago would be able to give to Michael as his son, seemed as good a time as any.

'I came back for— Why are you crying?' Alejandro rasped harshly as he came to a halt in the bedroom doorway.

Brynne looked up at him, unable not to notice how strong and handsome he looked, despite how she was feeling. She narrowed her eyes. 'Why do you think?' she snapped, resentful that this man, a man who made her pulse race in spite of herself, should witness the grief she was no longer able to contain.

His chin firmed squarely. 'I have no idea,' he said, shaking his head.

'No.' She straightened, her moment of weakness over as if she had been dowsed in icy-cold water. 'You wouldn't,' she scorned. 'What did you come back for?' she prompted quickly, wiping all trace of tears from her cheeks as she stood up to face him.

She had courage, this young woman, Alejandro acknowledged even as he felt discomforted by her crying.

She was very young, of course, ten years younger than his own thirty-five years, and in challenging him she had not chosen her fight wisely; once Alejandro was sure of Miguel's paternity, there had never been any doubt that he would claim the boy as his own.

Nevertheless, he was not completely unmoved by her tears, or the fact that her sadness gave her an air of fragile beauty, with her eyes now almost navy in colour against the pallor of her cheeks. Her red hair was lifted and secured off the long, creamy expanse of her neck to give her an air of vulnerability that had been evident in none of their previous encounters.

His mouth firmed. 'You are upset.' He stated the obvious. 'You perhaps wish for me to arrange for your immediate return to England?'

Her chin rose defiantly. 'You would like that, wouldn't you?'

His nostrils flared impatiently. 'I would like to put an end to these—disagreements, yes.'

'I'll just bet you would!' She gave a humourless laugh. 'No can do, sorry,' she added derisively. 'I intend staying on here for the duration!'

'*Dios mío*!' Alejandro bit out his frustration with her stubbornness, and his hands clenched at his sides. 'Do not try me too far, Brynne,' he warned harshly. 'I make a much better friend than I do an enemy!'

'Friend'? The word echoed incredulously in Brynne's head while she acknowledged that he had used her given name for the first time in their acquaintance. That familiarity aside, there was no way she and this man could ever be friends!

None of her male friends had ever set her senses singing in the way just being in this man's company did.

'I think you'll find, Alejandro, that so do I,' she came back smoothly, her blue eyes dark with challenge as she deliberately made use of his own first name in return.

A nerve pulsed in his tightly clenched jaw. 'You are here on sufferance only—'

'I don't appear to be the one who's suffering, Alejandro,' she taunted mockingly.

His grey eyes narrowed icily as he drew himself up to his full six feet three inches in height. 'Miguel has expressed a wish to swim in the pool. Perhaps you will be so good as to give me his bathing things?'

Michael…

Her anger left her as suddenly as it had erupted as she thought of the only reason she was here. And much as she enjoyed baiting Alejandro Santiago, that wasn't it!

'Of course,' she muttered, moving to unzip the case that contained the clothes she had packed so lovingly late last night when she and Michael had returned from visiting her parents. Several other boxes containing Michael's toys had been put aboard the jet earlier this morning, too, waiting to eventually be forwarded to Alejandro's home in mainland Spain.

In fact, everything that Michael possessed had been brought aboard that plane earlier today…

'Here,' she said as she held out Michael's brightly coloured swimming trunks, tears once again blurring her vision, although she was determined she wouldn't cry in front of Alejandro again. The man obviously only saw it as a weakness he could take advantage of if his offer to have her flown home immediately was anything to go by!

Was she going to cry again? Alejandro wondered, thinking how he never had known how to deal with a woman's tears, not even Francesca's during their brief but wholly unhappy marriage. With Brynne Sullivan he definitely found her anger the easier emotion to respond to.

His impatient gaze remained on Brynne's face as he reached out to take the swimming trunks, slightly missing his objective as his hand brushed lightly against hers.

And instantly received the equivalent of an electric shock up into his fingers and along the length of his arm!

He snatched the swimming trunks before moving his hand back abruptly, his lids half-lowered over his steel-grey eyes as he looked down his nose at her.

He found this woman intensely infuriating.

Irritating.

A nuisance he longed to be rid of.

And yet for that one split second he knew that he had been totally aware of her too, of the pale delicacy of her skin, of the blood flowing so smoothly beneath its surface, of the heat and inner throb of her very being, so much so that he could almost feel that blood pulsing through her veins.

Idiot!

He was hot, he was thirsty, and not a little tired of the verbal fencing that took place every time he was anywhere near this woman.

He stepped back. 'I will sit by the pool with Miguel until you come down to join him,' he said dismissively.

Brynne looked up at Alejandro from beneath her dark lashes. What had happened just now? Some sort of electric shock to add to her increasing awareness of him. It had been a moment, a very brief moment, when everything had seemed clearer, sharper, when it had almost felt as if she could feel and hear the beat of Alejandro's heart.

Which was pretty ridiculous when the man didn't have a heart!

If he did then he wouldn't continue to be so unreasonable where Michael was concerned, and would be as eager as she was to make all of this as painless as possible for his six-year-old son.

Besides, if he did have a heart, it would make her unwanted response to him all the more dangerous!

'I assume my joining you and Michael by the pool will no doubt free you to disappear on some important business or other?' she questioned.

The thinning of his sculpted lips showed his impatience. 'You already know I have business interests here,' he bit out curtly.

'Don't let us keep you from them, then,' Brynne taunted.

His eyes narrowed to silver slithers. 'You are a guest in my home, Brynne, and as such you will be treated with respect and courtesy. But as I warned you once before, do not push me too far, or you may not like the consequences!'

She probably wouldn't, Brynne acknowledged ruefully, having no doubts that Alejandro could make life a lot more uncomfortable for her than she could for him if he chose to do so. She was sure the slightly cruel curl she occasionally saw to his lips could very easily be put into action.

Except she had no intention of being in the least cowed by this man. 'I'll bear that in mind,' she drawled. 'Now, if you wouldn't mind, I would like to go through to my bedroom and unpack a few of my own things before coming down to the pool…' she dismissed.

A dismissal he definitely didn't like, by the look of his glittering eyes and the tensing of his shoulders as he strode forcefully from the room.

She was infuriated by the effect Alejandro Santiago had on her, and never felt in the least relaxed in his company. In fact, her skin seemed to prickle every time she was anywhere near him, almost as if she had been stung by nettles or lots of little insects.

She was also filled, at every opportunity, with a burning desire to shake him out of that cold arrogance with which he seemed to cloak himself.

Unless it wasn't a cloak…

But surely it had to be? Brynne simply couldn't see fun-loving Joanna having fallen for someone who was so cold and remote.

It had to be a shield of some sort, a way of hiding the man he was underneath.

At least, she hoped for Michael's sake that was what it was…

CHAPTER THREE

ALEJANDRO was glad he was wearing dark sunglasses to shield the surprise he felt when Brynne stepped out onto the terrace ten minutes later wearing only a very brief turquoise bikini.

It hadn't been apparent in the tailored trousers and fitted blouses she invariably wore, but, as Alejandro could quite clearly see now, Brynne Sullivan had a spectacularly beautiful body.

Absolutely, perfectly beautiful, with skin a creamy gold colour all over, her legs long and slender, hips curvaceous below her tiny waist, and her breasts pert beneath the clinging turquoise material.

But it was a beauty she seemed completely unaware of as she strolled across to where he sat, her hips swaying gracefully as she walked.

Alejandro, however, was very aware of it as he felt an unexpected throb in his own body!

'You're free to go now,' she told him coolly as she settled herself down on the lounger next to his.

Her scathing tone instantly dampened anything but the anger this woman always aroused in him. 'I intend to,' he snapped as he swung his feet down onto the tiled terrace. 'Dinner will be served at eight-thirty—'

'That's far too late for Michael,' she protested with a firm shake of her head.

It probably was, he acknowledged irritably, not having given too much thought to the changes Miguel was going to make to his daily routine. The fact that he had a son at all was still a source of surprise to him. Not that he thought for a moment that Brynne had even considered this—she seemed to think he was totally without emotions.

His reaction minutes ago to the way she looked in a bikini had told Alejandro quite the contrary!

But he did have several telephone calls to make before this evening's meal—at least one of which would no doubt be lengthy.

'Perhaps I can have a word with the cook so that she can prepare Michael something earlier than that?' Brynne decided to take pity on Alejandro's obvious frustration. 'Michael is usually in bed by eight o'clock.' Although that would no doubt be changed and adapted now that Michael was to take up a Mediterranean lifestyle...

But not tonight, she decided as she watched him swimming in the pool with the agility of a fish. He would be worn out by the early evening, and there had already been enough changes in his young life for one day. Michael needed some of his usual routine in order that everything shouldn't spiral completely out of control.

'That would be best, I think.' Alejandro gave an abrupt inclination of his head as he turned to leave.

'Tell me,' Brynne murmured dryly as she looked up at him, 'who was going to look after Michael if I hadn't been here?' she taunted.

Alejandro's mouth tightened. 'I had arranged for Maria's daughter—Maria is the cook,' he explained dismissively, '—to be with him.'

Brynne grimaced. 'Yet another stranger.'

'Brynne, you do not—' Alejandro broke off, frowning down at her, his jaw once again tight, which emphasized the haughty planes of his face. 'This is—new territory, for all of us,' he finally said quietly. 'I suggest that you give us all time to—adjust.'

'By "us" you presumably mean you,' she dismissed. 'I have been taking care of Michael quite capably for the last two months.'

Alejandro drew in a ragged breath. 'Do you intend arguing with me for the whole of your stay here?'

'Probably,' she replied; after all, Michael's welfare was all she was interested in.

Although she had to say that Alejandro Santiago seemed less—alien, in these surroundings, his dark good looks more suited to this climate. In fact, she was the one, with her red hair and pale complexion, who was out of place. Which was one of the reasons she felt increasingly defensive.

One of them.

The other one was the memory of that brief moment of physical awareness a short time ago between herself and Alejandro…

Alejandro found himself relaxing slightly as he gave a rueful inclination of his head. 'That is honest, anyway,' he drawled dryly.

'Oh, I believe you will invariably find me honest,' Brynne assured him.

'Good.' He nodded, smiling slightly as her raised

brows showed her surprise at his answer. 'Honesty is something I can deal with. It is dishonesty that I find unacceptable.' His mouth tightened grimly as he thought of all Francesca's lies and deceit, and of their marriage that had taught him never to trust a woman ever again. 'If you wish to telephone anyone to let them know of your safe arrival—'

'Anyone?' she echoed with a taunting smile.

'Your parents, possibly,' Alejandro answered slightly impatiently. 'I am sure they would like to know that you and Miguel have arrived here safely.'

Brynne's smile faded as she thought of her mother and father. Her mother had been ill with grief since Tom and Joanna had died so suddenly, and her father was having to deal with that as well as his own agony. The situation with Michael was completely beyond their comprehension at the moment.

A situation this man had created.

'I'm sure they would,' she acknowledged curtly.

Alejandro gave an abrupt nod of his head. 'Please feel free to use the telephone in the villa. I have a separate line in my study for business purposes.'

Brynne roused herself from her melancholy thoughts, her expression once again challenging as she looked up at him. 'Well, of course you do,' she muttered under her breath.

Alejandro's mouth tightened. 'I sincerely hope that this verbal fencing will not continue at mealtimes!'

'Oh, I think it probably will,' she returned wryly.

So the angry frustration Alejandro felt in the company of this woman was now to be accompanied by indigestion after every meal, too!

He thought longingly of his well-ordered life of two months ago. Before he had discovered Miguel was his son. Before the maddeningly outspoken Brynne Sullivan had entered, and then refused to leave, his life.

He nodded abruptly. 'As you wish.'

'Oh, it's not as I wish at all, Alejandro,' she told him derisively. 'You wouldn't be here if wishes really did come true!'

No one had ever spoken to him before in the way that this woman did, Alejandro realized irritably. The honesty he had praised earlier was one thing, but Brynne seemed to have no qualms whatsoever in saying whatever came into her head!

Her beautiful head, he accepted with a frown.

'Brynne—'

'Aunty Bry!' Michael greeted excitedly from the pool as he swam to the side to grin up at them, his dark hair slicked back from his face. 'Are you coming in, Aunty Bry?'

'Of course I am, darling.' With one last mocking lift of her brows in Alejandro's direction, Brynne moved gracefully to her feet, and reached up to pull the clip from her hair to let it fall loosely over her shoulders and down her spine.

Alejandro felt as if time stood still as he watched the wild tumble of titian locks. The sun caught their fiery silkiness, showing gold amongst the red, giving the effect of a living flame.

He knew Brynne was a schoolteacher, but she was unlike any schoolteacher he had ever known during his years of education!

'I will see you both later,' he snapped tersely before turning to stride forcefully back into the villa.

Work, he told himself firmly as he resisted the lure of staying by the swimming pool to watch Brynne and Miguel. He had been away for three days, and had numerous calls and messages waiting to be dealt with.

And that was before he even attempted to placate the other trouble-causing woman in his life—Antonia...!

'Well, isn't this cosy?' Brynne said dryly as she looked down the length of the dinner table to where her host sat in remote solitude at the other end of the twelve-foot-long table.

He looked magnificent, of course, if a little over-dressed for dining with someone he considered an un-welcome guest at best. The black evening suit and crisp snowy-white shirt gave his haughty good looks a rakish appeal she could well have done without.

Not having known whether or not she was supposed to dress for dinner, but having had a feeling that she probably was, Brynne was wearing what she considered her trusty little black dress, a light knee-length sheath of a dress with ribbon shoulder straps that complemented the light tan she had already managed to acquire during her hours beside the pool earlier today.

Michael, at least, was having a wonderful time in the novelty of his new home, and had fallen asleep within minutes of Brynne putting him to bed.

Her gaze narrowed on her host. 'Did you go up and say goodnight to Michael?'

Alejandro gave an inward sigh; dinner really was to

become as much a battleground as every other encounter with this woman!

'He had already fallen asleep by the time I went upstairs,' he said briskly, sure this was yet another black mark against him as far as Brynne Sullivan was concerned. The way her eyes flashed deeply blue told him he was right in his surmise.

'Then perhaps you should have gone upstairs earlier than you did,' she replied disapprovingly.

Critical as well as outspoken; it was not a comfortable combination in a woman!

'Perhaps I should,' he rasped. 'But—' He broke off in frustration as Maria arrived with their first course.

'Thank you,' Brynne said as she turned to smile at the tiny Majorcan woman. She had spent a pleasant hour in the kitchen with Maria earlier as Michael ate his tea, the two of them managing to converse a little in Brynne's schoolgirl Spanish and the small smattering of English the middle-aged woman had acquired from the tourists that flocked to this beautiful island every year.

The language barrier certainly hadn't been an obstacle to Maria's obvious affection for children as she had chatted to and smiled at Michael at every opportunity.

Brynne's smile faded as the tiny woman left the room and she turned to find Alejandro watching her with unreadable grey eyes. 'I'm sure Michael would like to see some of the island while I'm here, so perhaps I could have the use of a car tomorrow?' she suggested in a businesslike manner, having decided earlier that the novelty of the pool would wear off if that was all Michael had to do all day.

Besides, getting out and about on the island also

meant getting away from the unnervingly handsome Alejandro Santiago!

'I will put the limousine and driver at your disposal—'

'That's hardly the same as being able to drive myself about, now, is it?' Brynne protested, having eaten some of her starter of melon and ham and found it delicious.

Alejandro's gaze narrowed as he noted that her red hair was worn up again this evening, the flames tamed into muted fire with only a wispy fringe loose on her smooth brow. There was now a golden tan to her heart-shaped features, a peach gloss on the fullness of her lips, while the gentle arch of her neck was bare and the fragility of her slender body was emphasized by the fitted black dress.

'I would…prefer it if you allowed my driver to take you wherever you wish to go,' he said carefully.

Her blue eyes glittered with mockery. 'Don't you trust me not to disappear back to England with Michael?' she taunted.

Alejandro's mouth tightened. 'I would find you if you did,' he stated with certainty.

A frown creased her brow as she searched his face. 'I'll just bet that you would, too,' she finally murmured disgustedly.

'It is a bet you would win,' Alejandro drawled.

She eyed him in frustration. 'I would prefer to drive my own car so that the two of us are free to explore!'

'I have told you Juan will be happy to take you wherever you wish to go,' Alejandro assured firmly, having no intention of arguing any further with her on this point.

'So Michael and I are to be virtual prisoners while

we're here, is that it?' Brynne snapped as she put her knife and fork down on the plate and pushed it away from her, her appetite quickly disappearing.

Alejandro looked every inch the haughty Spaniard that he undoubtedly was as he gave her a quelling glance. 'It is not a question of making the two of you prisoners—'

'Then what is it a question of?' Brynne demanded as she sat forward, twin spots of angry colour in her cheeks.

He gave a disgruntled snort. 'You are a very difficult woman—'

'Difficult I can live with,' she assured him impatiently. 'It's being treated like a prisoner that I object to!'

Alejandro Santiago looked at her with obvious frustration for several seconds, his mouth in a thin disapproving line, his grey eyes glacial. 'Very well,' he finally said coldly. 'You may take a car and drive wherever you wish, but I cannot allow you to take Miguel about the island unprotected!'

Brynne stared at him incredulously. What on earth—?

'Miguel is my son, Brynne,' Alejandro snapped impatiently.

She frowned. 'Yes, but—'

'I am sure that when we arrived here you noted the electric gates and high fences as we came onto the property…'

'Well, yes…but—'

'There are also several security guards patrolling the property. Do not be so naïve, Brynne!' he bit out tautly as she continued to look puzzled. 'There have been several high-profile kidnappings in Europe in recent years. And my fight for custody of Miguel was very well publicized,' he reminded her quietly.

Brynne felt slightly sick as the full reality of what he was saying hit her. As he was the son of the super-wealthy Alejandro Santiago, there was a possibility that Michael could become a target for kidnappers!

She swallowed hard. 'But—I— Michael has been living with me quite openly for the last two months!'

Alejandro gave an abrupt inclination of his head. 'And he has been protected since I became aware of his existence,' he assured her arrogantly. 'Quietly. Unobtrusively. But, nevertheless, he has been protected.'

Brynne felt her cheeks pale. 'When he was at school…'

'Then too.' Alejandro gave another terse nod.

It was unbelievable. All this time, all those weeks, and she hadn't suspected a thing!

But that was the whole idea, wasn't it? she acknowledged. What was the point of being unobtrusively protected if everyone knew about it?

'That's—' She broke off, swallowing down her nausea. 'I had no idea! Why didn't you tell me?' she attacked angrily as her initial shock began to wear off.

Alejandro had been waiting for that, knowing Brynne wouldn't be virtually speechless for very long. 'There was no need for you to know—'

'Oh, and this is on a need-to-know basis, is it?' she retorted furiously. 'Michael could have been in danger any time during the last few weeks and you didn't think I needed to know!' She threw her napkin down on the table before standing up to walk down the length of the table to stand next to him. 'You arrogant…!'

He shrugged without concern, his grey gaze coldly

unyielding as he looked up at her. 'I merely protect what is mine.'

Without telling her there was any need for that protection… How she despised this man!

CHAPTER FOUR

'WOULD you and Miguel like to come for a drive to Deya with me…?'

Brynne glanced up from the magazine she had been looking through while Michael once again frolicked about in the pool, her eyes hidden behind dark sunglasses as she looked up at Alejandro.

If uncovered they would definitely have told Alejandro that her anger towards him hadn't abated in the least since she had stormed out of the dining-room the evening before!

It was an anger she wanted to cling to, finding it a much more comfortable emotion than her physical awareness of this man. Today he was casually dressed again in black trousers and a grey shirt that emphasized his dark colouring.

Her mouth twisted derisively. 'And what's in Deya?'

'Nothing too exciting,' he acknowledged dryly. 'But while I attend a business meeting you and Miguel could have a look around the village, and then perhaps we could all meet up for lunch.'

'What's the catch?' She eyed him suspiciously.

Alejandro was starting to regret making the invitation. 'There is no catch,' he snapped. 'I was merely thinking of your request yesterday to see some of the island.'

'And I suppose Michael and I are to be accompanied by armed guards wearing dark sunglasses and looking totally out of place?' she queried sarcastically.

His mouth tightened. 'They are not armed,' he responded tautly.

'But they will be wearing dark sunglasses and looking out of place!' Brynne scorned as she swung her legs onto the tiled patio, and Alejandro noted she was wearing a black bikini today that suited the golden tan she was quickly acquiring.

Alejandro eyed her impatiently. 'You are being extremely childish about this—'

'Am I?' she challenged. 'Well, I'm terribly sorry about that! But it could be because this is the first time I've ever had to be accompanied anywhere by guards—armed or otherwise!' Although she knew Alejandro saw it as a necessary tool to keep Michael safe, she certainly didn't agree with the way he had gone about it.

He had realized that after their brief conversation on the subject last night, and he had tried to make allowances for it, but at the same time he did not intend fighting this woman over everything.

'I suggest, for the length of your stay here, you get used to it!' he said harshly.

She was arguing for the sake of it, Brynne acknowledged heavily. She still wasn't happy with the idea that Michael would now need to be watched and protected wherever he went, but at the same time she accepted that it was better than Alejandro not caring enough about Michael to keep him safe.

As for herself, she had no intention of getting used to being watched all the time!

She gave Alejandro Santiago one last scathing glance before turning to look at Michael as he swam over to hang on the side of the pool. 'Your father has invited us to go for a drive with him to a place called Deya,' she prompted softly, having no intention of making Michael a part of the tension that seemed to surround his father and herself every time they met; after all, she was here to smooth the way for a relationship between the two, not make the situation any worse than it already was.

Although Michael didn't seem to be having too much trouble adjusting, last night being the first time he hadn't woken up crying for Joanna and Tom.

Her own evening hadn't been quite so untroubled, she thought. Sha had sat out on the balcony of her bedroom still trying to calm down after her argument with Alejandro when she had seen him leave the villa to walk over to the garages, driving a sleek sports car out onto the road minutes later, the red tail-lights quickly disappearing down the winding road as he had accelerated the vehicle away.

She remembered thinking ten o'clock at night seemed an odd time to be going out...

Although it perhaps explained why he had been so formally dressed for dinner earlier. Maybe it hadn't been in her honour at all, but because he'd had another—assignation, later that evening?

She knew from their legal battle over Michael that Alejandro didn't have a wife or a fiancée, but that didn't mean that he didn't have a particular woman in his life.

Not that it was any of her business, she had told herself firmly. No matter what Alejandro might have assumed to the contrary, she intended continuing to be a part of Michael's life even after this month was finished. But at the same time she accepted she had no right, legal or otherwise, to comment on whom Alejandro might possibly one day choose to be Michael's stepmother.

'What do you think?' she prompted Michael brightly now.

'Great!' He grinned, easily levering himself up out of the water to grab a towel and hurry into the villa to dress.

Brynne's heart caught in her throat as she watched him, aware that the sun here was already darkening his skin to the same olive of his natural father, and that Michael seemed to be becoming more and more like Alejandro Santiago with each passing hour.

'I think that's a yes.' Her voice was brittle as she spoke dismissively to Alejandro. 'We'll just change and then join you back down here,' she added before turning to pick up her book and magazine with the intention of joining Michael upstairs.

'I forgot to enquire yesterday evening—your parents were both well when you spoke to them yesterday?' Alejandro asked softly.

She straightened abruptly, her expression tense. 'As well as can be expected, in the circumstances.'

Yes, Alejandro could only imagine his own parents' distress if anything were to happen to himself or his brother.

Or his own distress, even now, if anything should happen to Miguel...

He had only spent a few hours in the little boy's

company, but already he knew him to be strong and independent, his nature naturally cheerful in spite of his recent loss, with none of the spoilt whining that sometimes happened with children.

Miguel was a boy he recognized as being very like himself at the age of six. A boy he was already proud of.

Although no doubt Brynne Sullivan, believing him cold and heartless, would find that hard to believe!

'It must be very difficult for them,' Alejandro recognized.

'Yes,' Brynne agreed. 'Taking Michael to see them the night before we left was—harrowing.'

Alejandro knew this was far from an ideal situation, that the discovery of his son had far-reaching consecquences, not least to the couple who considered themselves his grandparents.

But there was no easy solution to this dilemma that Alejandro could see.

'We won't be long,' Brynne told him shortly.

'I am in no particular hurry.' Alejandro shrugged, watching her walk back to the house before sitting down wearily on one of the loungers to wait for them. Allowing his head to fall back on the cushion and his eyes to close, he thought how Antonia had been particularly difficult last night, so much so that in the end he had cut the evening short and driven home much earlier than he had intended.

He accepted that the time he'd had to spend in England the last six weeks had been time spent away from Majorca, but it was a separation that Antonia had felt much more personally than he had. As her displeasure had clearly let him know last night. Even her exotic beauty did not compensate for the air of possessiveness she had started to adopt where he was concerned. A possessiveness she had no right to feel.

Why did women become so highly strung?

Well…women like the possessive Antonia and the faithless Francesca, he conceded ruefully. He somehow couldn't see Brynne Sullivan resorting to hysterics, or tears, in order to get her own way.

He was more likely to feel the sharp edge of her tongue if—he stopped himself quickly.

What was he doing thinking of Brynne in that way, when the chances of the two of them ever indulging in an affair—which was all he had to offer any woman now—were precisely nil?

There had been many affairs since Francesca's death five years ago, brief, transitional relationships that hadn't even dented the air of self-preservation he had adopted after his disastrous marriage.

Alejandro gave a self-derisive shake of his head, knowing that Brynne was the one woman he need never fear he would ever become involved with. She was far too emotional, and since the complete failure of his marriage emotion was something he had avoided like the plague the last five years.

Besides, the two of them disliked each other intensely!

Coming back outside with Michael a few minutes later, Brynne hung back slightly as she took in Alejandro's totally relaxed pose on the lounger.

His face looked younger and more classically handsome when not dominated by those fierce silver-grey eyes, and she was struck once again by how lethally attractive he was.

Or would be—if she didn't dislike him so much!

He did look a little tired this morning though, and after witnessing his nocturnal roaming the night before, she didn't need too many guesses as to the reason why.

He might not have a wife or a fiancée, but after his disappearance the evening before Brynne didn't doubt that he had a 'something'! Nor did she doubt that her own and Michael's presence here made absolutely no difference to the continuance of that relationship.

'I thought we were going out?' she reminded sharply.

Alejandro drew in a deeply controlling breath before raising his eyebrows. One thing it was definitely not possible to do in this woman's company was relax!

Especially when she was wearing a green halter-top that revealed the creamy cleft between her breasts and a pair of brief white shorts that showed the long expanse of her bare legs.

'We are,' he said firmly as he stood up, leaving Brynne to follow behind while he walked over to the garages with Miguel. He was annoyed with himself for even noticing Brynne's leggy beauty, although he dared any red-blooded man not to do so!

He drove them to Deya himself, knowing from Miguel's grinning face in the back of the Mercedes that he was enjoying driving along with the roof down, and having his dark hair blown about by the wind.

It was much more difficult to gauge Brynne's reaction to the magnificent views they encountered on the drive, her eyes once again behind dark sunglasses, and her expression unreadable.

No doubt her thoughts were yet another criticism of himself!

Nothing he did, it seemed, found favour from her,

with his every word and every action viewed with distrust or derision.

It was not a response he was used to in a woman!

Since the age of sixteen, his dark looks had enabled Alejandro to take his pick of women, and with maturity had come the added bonus of being an entrepreneurial multimillionaire. The wealth and power of such a position seemed an added aphrodisiac to many women.

But Brynne Sullivan seemed to detest him for those attributes!

'How do you like the island so far?' he asked, attempting conversation.

'It's very beautiful,' she replied stiltedly.

'Many artists live in Deya. Some good. Some not so good,' he allowed dryly. 'I am sure you will enjoy looking in the galleries there.'

'Maybe,' she conceded with a shrug of her bare shoulders. 'Did you put your guards in the boot of the car?' she enquired derisively.

Alejandro's expression darkened at her deliberate challenge. He was trying to be pleasant, so why couldn't this woman at least attempt to meet him halfway?

'Raul and Rafael are in the car behind,' he muttered softly.

Brynne glanced in the wing mirror of the Mercedes, easily spotting the dark vehicle driving thirty metres or so behind them.

'How nice,' she responded tartly. 'Perhaps we can all have coffee together once we get to Deya!'

'Why do you persist—' Alejandro broke off his angry rebuke, his mouth thinning disapprovingly as he glanced at Miguel in the driver mirror. 'We cannot get there soon enough for me,' he muttered so that only Brynne Sullivan could hear him, her mocking smile his only answer.

Not surprisingly the two of them spent the rest of the journey in silence, although both of them had conversations with Michael as he asked a barrage of questions about his new surroundings.

Thank goodness for Michael, Brynne thought ruefully.

Although, without Michael, she would never have met the nerve-tinglingly handsome Alejandro Santiago in the first place...

There really weren't too many Spanish multimillionaires roaming the streets of Cambridge, she thought wryly.

She had dated on and off over the years, other students, fellow teachers, all of them without exception nice, pleasant men whom she had enjoyed spending time with.

In the six stormy weeks she had known Alejandro Santiago she already knew he was neither nice nor pleasant.

As for enjoying his company...how could she possibly relax enough to do that when just sitting beside him like this made her feel hot all over?

'Deya,' Alejandro announced with a certain amount of relief as he parked the Mercedes outside one of the village's most prestigious hotels, intending to have lunch here with Miguel and Brynne once his business meeting was over.

Although he doubted Brynne would be impressed by the exclusive charms of the hotel, let alone the excellence of the restaurant. She seemed to find little merit to any of the luxurious lifestyle his money provided!

'I will book lunch here for one o'clock,' he told her as he came round to open the car door for her before tilting the seat forward so that Miguel could climb out of the back.

Her head tilted as she looked up at him through her dark shades. 'I'm sure Raul and Rafael will ensure that we don't get lost,' she drawled with a mocking glance in the direction of the two men getting out of the black car parked a short distance away.

Alejandro damped down his rising anger with effort. His meeting was an important one, crucial to the delicate negotiations that brought him to the island at this time, and allowing this constant discord with Brynne Sullivan to sabotage those negotiations by going to his meeting angry and impatient was not an option.

'I am sure that they will,' he acknowledged tautly. 'Take care of your aunt, Miguel,' he added, his hand on his son's shoulders, his expression softening as he looked down at him.

Miguel grinned up at him. 'Aunty Bry usually looks after me.'

Alejandro gave an acknowledging inclination of his head. 'In Spain it is the man who takes care of the woman,' he explained gravely.

'Oh.' Miguel nodded his head understandingly.

Brynne gave an irritated frown. Michael was six years old, for goodness' sake—

'It is as well that Miguel learns the Spanish way,' Alejandro declared.

She raised her chin as her gaze met the challenge in his cold grey eyes. 'I'm sure there's a lot we can all learn from one another's cultures,' she said non-committally, knowing by the way Alejandro's gaze narrowed that the double-edge to her reply wasn't lost on him.

He gave an impatient shrug. 'You will need some euros—'

'I have my own money, thank you,' Brynne cut in sharply as Alejandro would have reached into his trouser pocket.

He raised his dark brows. 'I was talking to Miguel.'

'I have enough for Michael, too,' she assured him, her anger barely contained. She might only be a lowly schoolteacher, but that didn't mean she was going to accept money, even on Michael's behalf, from this man! 'Please don't let us delay you any longer from your meeting,' she added with saccharine sweetness.

Alejandro continued to look at her impatiently for several long seconds before giving a dismissive shake of his head. 'One o'clock,' he bit out tersely before turning away.

Brynne was determined to forget about Alejandro Santiago, and his arrogance for the next couple of hours as she and Michael wandered around the pretty village. The people were so friendly, with men and women alike smiling and talking to Michael in the shops and café they stopped in to have a cool drink.

They were not joined by Raul and Rafael, thank goodness, although the two men were loitering outside waiting for them when they came out of the café half an hour later.

Michael, luckily, seemed completely unaware of the men's presence, holding her hand and skipping along happily at her side as they made their way back.

'Alej—Father is nice, don't you think, Aunty Bry?'

He looked up at her a little anxiously as they walked up the steps to the hotel.

'Nice' was the last thing Alejandro Santiago was!

But Michael's question showed that he wasn't as unaware of the animosity between Brynne and his father as she could have wished. Not surprisingly, really, when that antagonism surfaced every time the two of them were together. But it wasn't good for Michael to have noticed it and so have his loyalties pulled in two different directions in this way.

'Very nice,' she told him brightly.

Michael frowned. 'Did Mummy and Daddy like him, do you think?'

Brynne gave a pained frown. No doubt Joanna had 'liked' Alejandro Santiago seven years ago, but whether or not she would have still liked the man he was today Brynne had no idea. As for Tom, Brynne really had no idea what her brother would have made of this arrogantly assured man who was Michael's real father!

But that wasn't an answer she could give Michael. The little boy's future lay with Alejandro, whether she liked it or not, and loving Michael as she did it was up to her to make this change in his life as easy as possible for him.

If only she didn't find Alejandro so overwhelming physically!

'I'm sure they did,' she told Michael warmly as she gave his hand a reassuring squeeze, hoping Alejandro would appreciate her efforts—against her real feelings on the matter!—on his behalf.

'Good.' Michael sighed his relief.

Obviously Michael, even if he still didn't really understand how it had happened, was nevertheless getting used to the idea of having Alejandro as his father, and that had to be a good thing.

Even if Brynne couldn't share his enthusiasm!

She was even more disconcerted, when they reached the outdoor restaurant, to find that Alejandro wasn't sitting alone at the table they were being shown to. Instead a ravishingly beautiful woman sat beside him, her dark hair long and luxurious, her complexion as olive as his own and her exquisite features dominated by huge dark eyes and a pouting, red-painted mouth…

CHAPTER FIVE

ALEJANDRO'S mouth tightened slightly as he saw Brynne and Miguel being shown to the table where he and Antonia were sitting.

Antonia was not supposed to have been here with her father today, and Alejandro was annoyed that her unexpected presence had changed the meeting from any serious talk of business to yet another social occasion.

Deliberately or accidentally, on the part of Felipe Roig…?

It had been all too easy to flatter Antonia, the daughter of widower Felipe Roig, as a way of charming the older man. But if the way Antonia had begun to actively pursue him was any indication, it was a flattery she had begun to take all too seriously. Which could, in itself, lead to Felipe wanting a much bigger price for the land he had to sell than Alejandro was willing to pay…!

Not that Antonia wasn't beautiful. With a voluptuous figure that indicated a passionate nature she would no doubt more than satisfy the man lucky enough to become her husband—it just wouldn't be Alejandro!

He and Francesca had married for all the wrong reasons, and their union had been painful as well as disastrous; he did not intend repeating the mistake!

It was a problem that Alejandro had had no chance to turn his mind to as Antonia had continued to linger long after her father had departed, but he had managed to avoid inviting Antonia to stay for lunch.

Although now that Brynne and Miguel had actually arrived at the restaurant he might no longer have any other choice!

He stood up as Brynne and Miguel reached the table, his smile less warm than he would have wished. 'Did you have an enjoyable morning?' he enquired politely.

'Oh, it was wonderful,' his son was the one to answer brightly. 'We went to all the shops, and then to a café where the man gave me a biscuit to eat with my juice, and we sat outside and watched as people filled huge water bottles from the stream that runs down from the mountains, and—'

'Slowly, Miguel, slowly.' Alejandro laughed as he halted his son's excited chatter, all the time aware that Brynne was looking at him with those questioning blue eyes before she glanced at Antonia and then back again. 'Miguel, I would like you to meet a friend of mine, Antonia Roig.' He placed his hands on Miguel's shoulders as he turned him to look at the woman sitting at the table. 'Antonia, this is—'

'Your son,' Antonia finished throatily, standing up as she curved her pouting red lips into a smile. 'But of course it is.' She nodded. 'He very much has the look of you, Alejandro.' Her smile warmed intimately as she looked up at him.

Brynne watched the exchange with growing trepidation. It was one thing to acknowledge that Alejandro was Michael's father but the little boy was only just coming to that understanding—surely this arrogant Spaniard wasn't going to introduce him to a stepmother quite so soon?

Antonia Roig was certainly beautiful enough, Brynne recognized as she looked at the tempestuous perfection of the other woman's face. But there was just something about the woman's eyes, a certain lack of warmth when she smiled, that indicated to Brynne that this woman might think 'boarding-school was a good idea' for any child that wasn't her own.

Although with Antonia's curvaceously alluring figure Brynne very much doubted that Alejandro's interest had gone as high as Antonia's eyes!

Antonia's deep brown gaze now narrowed on Brynne. 'How very sensible of you, Alejandro, to have brought Miguel's nanny, too.' She gave Brynne a politely dismissive smile before turning away. 'Alejandro, why do we not—'

'Oh, but Brynne isn't my nanny!' Michael dismissed with a laugh, totally unaware of any tension amongst the three adults. 'She's my aunty. My Aunty Bry,' he added happily.

Yes, very hard eyes, Brynne decided wryly as the other woman's deep brown orbs were turned back on her, with critical assessment this time as Antonia took in her appearance from the top of her red head to the soles of her white flip-flops, before returning to Brynne's make-upless face with its covering of freckles.

'Your…aunt,' Antonia finally murmured speculatively before glancing back at Alejandro, her dark, highly arched, plucked brows raised questioningly. 'The same aunt who…'

Obviously Alejandro hadn't had the chance yet to tell his…this woman that he had brought Michael's troublesome aunt back to Majorca for a visit too.

Oh dear!

'The same aunt,' Brynne told Antonia happily as she held out her hand. 'Brynne Sullivan. Are you joining us for lunch, Miss Roig?' she prompted lightly as the other woman met the gesture with the slightest brush of her slender, scarlet-tipped fingers.

The pouting red mouth tightened slightly. 'I would have, but unfortunately I have another engagement in Palma early this afternoon,' Antonia snapped dismissively. 'You have not forgotten that you are expected for dinner this evening, Alejandro?' she added tartly.

Oh, dear, dear, dear, Brynne mused as she sat down in the seat the other woman had just vacated; poor Alejandro looked as if he might have some explaining to do later!

'Of course I have not forgotten,' he confirmed, a little impatiently, Brynne thought as he brushed his lips lightly against the other woman's cheek in parting.

'What a pity Miss Roig couldn't join us,' Brynne remarked dryly once Antonia had left.

Alejandro turned from watching Antonia's abrupt departure to scowl down at Brynne's bent head as she perused the menu with marked deliberation. 'Yes, a pity,' he bit out tersely as he resumed his seat at the table, knowing by the way Brynne returned his gaze with wide-eyed innocence that she was enjoying what she no doubt sensed was his slight discomfort.

But what could he have done otherwise? To press

Antonia to join them would, with Brynne in this mischievously troublemaking mood, only have resulted in even more embarrassment, he was sure. No, he had done the right thing; he would have plenty of time to explain, and placate Antonia later tonight.

'It all looks delicious. What do you recommend?' Brynne asked as she closed the menu to look at him enquiringly, the mischief still dancing in those deep blue eyes.

She didn't look much older than Miguel with that innocent expression, her face bare of make-up, and her hair pulled back into a green band that matched the colour of her top.

Except that expression was too innocent!

'Everything,' he dismissed impatiently before turning his attention to helping Miguel select his food.

Surprisingly Brynne enjoyed the leisurely lunch. She and Alejandro spent most of the time ignoring each other—which had to be a definite plus as far as her digestion was concerned!—but Michael was starting to relax in his father's company and the food was excellent. The wine Alejandro ordered complemented their lunch perfectly, and the view was spectacular from where they sat high up on one of the terraces that looked down the valley to the sea.

In fact, by the time they left to drive back to the villa she was the most relaxed since arriving in Majorca.

Michael was quite happy to return to the pool in the afternoon, leaving Brynne to laze on one of the loungers as she pondered the merits of the local siesta; she could quite cheerfully have fallen asleep for an hour or so after that lovely meal and wine.

Although Alejandro's presence on the lounger beside her own pretty much assured her that she would never be able to relax enough to do that!

'So you're going out again this evening?' she prompted conversationally as she sat up to rub oil onto her tanning arms and legs.

'Again...?' Alejandro echoed softly as he turned to watch her movements, her fingers long and supple as she smoothed the oil into her shoulders and throat.

Brynne didn't even glance at him as she bent to rub oil on the long length of her legs. 'I saw you go out yesterday evening.' She shrugged.

But she obviously hadn't seen, or heard, him come back again two hours later...

His departure alone had obviously been enough for her to draw her own conclusions. And meeting Antonia today would certainly not have belied that conclusion.

Although why this woman should think she had any right to comment on what he did in his private life was beyond him!

He found his attention caught and held as Brynne pushed her halter-top up to just below her breasts as she now put oil onto her bare midriff. A completely flat midriff, with soft and creamy skin, and just a tanatalizing glimpse of the thrusting swell of her breasts beneath the green top—

What was he doing?

This woman was Miguel's aunt by marriage, his nuisance of an aunt by marriage, not someone whose attractions Alejandro should find in the least arousing.

His mouth tightened. 'You have a comment you wish to make about my dinner engagement?' he rasped hastily, all the time knowing that impatience was aimed at himself more than at Brynne.

She was a constant thorn in his side, an irritant he couldn't wait to be rid of, so what did it matter if she had a lithely beautiful body and that her skin looked like silk? Even the freckles that covered the whole of her body added to her sensuousness as he imagined discovering, and kissing, every single one of them...

'Not at all.' Brynne looked surprised by his question. 'I was just making conversation, Alejandro,' she dismissed lightly.

Like hell she was!

But he was not involved with Antonia in the way that Brynne seemed to think he was. Deliberately so. Flattering and charming Antonia was one thing, but he never, ever mixed business with the sort of pleasure he had been thinking of with Brynne herself a few minutes ago.

Although that slight possessiveness Antonia seemed to be developing where he was concerned told him that he might not have been his usual careful self where relationships were concerned during his distraction over the custody of Miguel. Both Antonia and her father might be expecting something more from the interest he had shown Antonia.

But he had no intention of ever going through the painful process of marrying again. And now that he had an heir in Miguel, he had no need to do so.

But there was still the problem of Felipe Roig's elusiveness...

He stood up quickly. 'I have some calls to make.'

'My, what a busy man you are, Alejandro,' Brynne looked up to taunt, her chin resting on her bent knee.

His gaze was cold as he looked down at her. 'I have business commitments, yes,' he replied coolly.

Brynne raised her eyebrows. 'How pleasant for you when the business is as beautiful as Antonia Roig.'

Alejandro's jaw clenched. 'Not that it is any of your concern, but my only connection with Antonia is business with her father, Felipe.'

'Really?' Brynne derided. 'That wasn't the impression I got!'

'I do not care—' Alejandro broke off his angry retort, breathing deeply as he looked down his arrogant nose at her. 'You really do not have the right to question me in this way, Brynne,' he finally snapped coldly.

'But the two of you are having dinner together this evening,' she challenged, not prepared to let him off that easily. After all, if he was considering making Antonia his wife, and consequently Michael's stepmother, then she did consider it her business!

'I am one of several guests invited for dinner this evening at the home of Antonia's father, yes,' he bit out impatiently.

'Ah…' she murmured speculatively, enjoying seeing this usually perfectly controlled man at a disadvantage for a change.

Alejandro scowled darkly. 'You really are the most— unsettling, of women!'

Brynne smiled. 'I'll take that as a compliment.'

'I would not,' he snarled, his accent becoming more pronounced in his obvious displeasure. 'So far I have not found being with you a restful experience!'

Her smile turned to a chuckle. 'I believe that's the nicest thing you've ever said to me, Alejandro!'

She was infuriating, Alejandro acknowledged, not for the first time. Infuriating, outspoken, and far too familiar.

But at the same time he also knew that he had never found a moment's boredom in this woman's company, either…

For a man who had been soured towards love years ago, his relationships since that time only having ever been on a physical level, it wasn't just unsettling to realize this, it was extremely disturbing!

He shook his head. 'I really do have to go and make some calls. What now?' he questioned in frustration as he saw Brynne's disapproving expression.

She shrugged. 'I was merely wondering if you ever intended to spend any time with Michael?'

Alejandro's frown darkened to a scowl. 'I have just finished having lunch with both of you.'

'Eating together and actually spending time together are two totally different things,' Brynne dismissed evenly.

He drew in a controlling breath. No one, absolutely no one, ever questioned him in this way!

'Tell me, Brynne,' he said tersely, 'have you ever been present at the taming of a wild stallion?'

Brynne gave him a puzzled glance. 'I can't say that I have.'

He nodded abruptly. 'Then if you had you would know that it takes patience. That first you have to let the stallion slowly become accustomed to your presence, to the sound of your voice. Once you have done that, you can begin to touch the stallion as you talk to it. Again this takes time. But once he accepts these things it is time to put on the saddle and bit. Only to put it on, you understand. It will take many more days before you can actually attempt to get up into the saddle. If you try to go too fast, to force these things, then you will break the animal rather than tame it.'

Brynne stared at him incredulously. 'Are you trying to tell me that you're treating getting to know Michael the same as taming a wild stallion?' she gasped disbelievingly.

He shrugged those broad shoulders. 'It is a tried and tested method.'

'You—you—' Her cheeks were flushed, her eyes bright with temper as she stood up to face him. 'Is that how you tame a woman too, Alejandro?' she challenged in disgust. 'Do you talk softly to them? Touch them? Caress them? Before taking them to your bed?' She was breathing hard in her agitation.

His jaw was tightly clenched, his pale grey eyes cold with anger as he glared down at her. 'You have no right—'

'I have every right if that's really the way you think you're going to get close to Michael!' she replied. 'You're incredible, do you know that?' She gave a disbelieving shake of her head. 'Absolutely incredible, if you think you can treat the emotions of a vulnerable little boy as lightly as you would the taming of a wild stallion!'

A nerve pulsed in that tightly clenched jaw. 'And you, Brynne, have never even tried to understand how difficult this situation is for me—'

'Forgive me, Alejandro,' she came back sarcastically. 'But you really aren't my first priority!'

'As well as Miguel,' Alejandro finished angrily. 'In fact, I believe you take delight in thinking the worst of me!' he snapped.

'I would think badly of any man who evaded his responsibilities for six years!' she retorted.

His eyes narrowed dangerously. 'So now we come to the true reason for your obvious contempt for me!'

'I've never even tried to pretend I feel anything else!' Brynne scorned.

He looked at her icily. 'You have no knowledge of what happened between Joanna and myself seven years ago!'

'I know enough,' Brynne assured him scathingly. 'Joanna didn't even trust you enough to tell you of her pregnancy, let alone try to include you in it!'

Alejandro's chest rose and fell rapidly as he tried to control his own temper, and tell himself that Brynne spoke out of ignorance rather than fact. She judged him on what she thought she knew rather than on what had actually happened seven years ago.

It didn't work, his anger not abating in the slightest. 'I advise you not to make judgements on something you do not understand,' he told her coldly.

'Oh, I understand you only too well, Alejandro,' Brynne assured him with a disgusted toss of her head, blue eyes glittering. 'You're cold. You're aloof. And your all-knowing arrogance is just unbelievable!'

He continued to look at her in frustration for several long seconds, his jaw clamped tightly together as he debated whether he wanted to verbally tear Brynne apart, or just pull her into his arms and kiss her until she was senseless.

The latter emotion won!

He reached out to pull her slender body into his and felt the softness of her skin against his own as he held her tightly against him and took possession of the sensuous curve of her lips.

The kiss was so unexpected, so fiercely hot, that Brynne had no chance to do anything other than respond.

It was like drowning! Every part of her seemed to melt into Alejandro, her hands moving up as she clung to the broad width of his shoulders.

And then Alejandro was pushing her away from him, a nerve pulsing in his tightly clenched jaw when he turned back from ensuring that Michael hadn't seen the exchange. He hadn't.

'I have to go,' he finally muttered determinedly before turning on his heel and striding purposefully back to the villa, his back and shoulders rigid.

Brynne watched him go, very much aware of the fact that, instead of repulsing Alejandro's kisses, the ache in her body told her she actually regretted that they had ended so soon…!

CHAPTER SIX

BRYNNE shifted on the bed as she tried to find a comfortable position in which to fall asleep.

Something she had been trying to do for the last hour, feeling too restless to settle down to read the book she had brought away with her, and Alejandro not having returned from his evening out yet.

She had been so angry with him this afternoon, then so surprised and aroused as he had kissed her.

In fact, she had been so distracted, so disturbed, that she had felt relieved when Maria had come out and offered to take Michael for a walk to the village with her.

But the result was that Brynne had been so worn out from puzzling over that kiss, her head so full of the things she should have said to Alejandro and hadn't, that she had eventually fallen into a deep sleep as she had continued to lay on the lounger beside the pool.

Only to wake up an hour later to find her back sunburnt because she had been too agitated earlier to remember to put any oil on it before falling asleep.

Brynne got impatiently out of the bed, the after-sun she had managed to put on her shoulders earlier, and partway up her back, doing absolutely nothing to alleviate the heat or the stinging sensation that continued to keep her from sleeping.

She opened the French doors to stroll out onto the balcony, hearing the distant clanging of a bell around the neck of a goat or sheep, and the clicking sound of the cicadas.

The island really was beautiful, with the brightly coloured bougainvillea that grew in such abundance, the orange and lemon trees that grew on the terraced hillsides and the tiny villages with their wondrous smells of cooking, old-fashioned shops and cafés. Plus it was all surrounded by the most magnificently coloured sea Brynne had ever seen.

But it was all ruined for Brynne by the presence of Alejandro.

What had happened between the two of them earlier today?

She wasn't quite sure…

The conversation had started out so innocently. And ended in that fiercely heated kiss, a kiss that had left such tension and disharmony between them that Brynne had felt restless and disturbed ever since.

Because she was still angry with him, she had told herself after he had left her. It was only when she had come up to bed, and sleep had continued to elude her, that she had allowed her thoughts to become less angry, to try to understand why their conversation had deteriorated in the way that it had, with the result that Alejandro had actually kissed her.

Her conclusion, at least as far as she was concerned, was not a pleasant one!

There had been such intensity between them during that heated exchange, so that when he had kissed her so suddenly her body had given her no choice but to respond. At which point she had been totally aware of the heat of him, of the broadness of his shoulders, of the hard power—and pleasure—that hardness promised—

No!

Brynne closed her eyes to shut out the memory. It would be extremely stupid on her part to allow her sexual awareness of Alejandro to get any deeper than it already was.

But what if it was something she had no control over?

She could hear the sound of a car coming down the narrow, winding road to the villa, and knew it had to be Alejandro returning from his evening out.

There was something slightly undignified about the possibility that Alejandro might see her standing out on the balcony and think she had been waiting here for him to come home.

She hadn't, had she…?

It didn't matter whether she had or not, she decided as she moved quickly back into her bedroom and shut the door behind her; Alejandro wasn't going to see her and jump to any conclusion, erroneous or otherwise.

Sounds carried in the silence of the night, and she heard Alejandro park the car in the garage, then the scrape of his shoes on the terrace as he walked to the villa and let himself in.

Her nerves tensed as she waited for him to ascend the stairs and walk down the hallway as he went to bed.

The light knock on her bedroom door startled her so

much she almost knocked over the vase of lilies that stood on her dressing table.

Alejandro had come to her bedroom, not his own!

Because of that kiss they had shared this afternoon? Had Alejandro realized that part of her anger towards him had been because she had been inexplicably roused by the exchange?

You're being stupid now, Brynne, she instantly rebuked her panicked thoughts. As far as Alejandro was concerned she had told him how much she didn't like him this afternoon.

'Yes?' she called out, lacing her fingers together to stop them from trembling.

The door opened slowly, and Alejandro came quietly into the room. 'I saw the light was still on in your bedroom and wondered if there was a problem…?' He arched his dark brows.

Yes, there was a problem, Brynne realized achingly as she felt her nipples harden beneath her silky pyjamas from just looking at him in his evening suit, the warmth of her body centred between her thighs now.

The darkness of his hair was slightly ruffled by the evening breeze, and the top button of his shirt was undone to reveal the beginning of the dark hair that no doubt covered his chest and went down to his—

She lifted her startled gaze back up to his face and instantly wished that she hadn't as she found her eyes were now held and captured by the intensity of his.

'Brynne…?' he prompted.

She swallowed hard, inwardly chastising herself for her stupidity. 'Er—no, there's no problem,' she answered him determinedly. 'I—just couldn't sleep, that's all. It's—very hot this evening, isn't it?'

Hotter still since Alejandro had entered her bedroom!

What was wrong with her? She wasn't an impressionable teenager but a mature woman of twenty-five, and had been out with a number of men over the last few years—

But none of them had been in the least like Alejandro!

No, they had been nice men, ordinary men, men who had shared her interests, men she had been able to talk to, not a man who filled a room just by walking into it, a man who could command with just a look, a man who had upset and disturbed her life since the moment he had entered it six weeks ago, a man who—

A man who created a moist heat between her thighs just by being in the same room as her!

This was awful.

Terrible.

'Brynne, what—'

'No!' she exclaimed when she saw he was about to walk farther into her bedroom. 'It's late, Alejandro,' she told him abruptly. 'I would like to go back to bed now.'

Alejandro searched her face. Was he being ridiculous? Brynne had looked at him just now as if—well, as if she returned some of the desire he had felt when he had kissed her this afternoon.

It was a feeling he had tried to dismiss as fanciful after he'd left her, and then again this evening as he had sat at the crowded dinner table of the Roigs, Antonia's attempts to tease him out of his reverie completely unsuccessful. In fact, he had felt himself becoming more and more impatient this evening with Antonia's attempts to beguile him with her sultry beauty!

He had seen the light still on in Brynne's bedroom as he had driven down the hill to the villa and had told himself not to knock on her door. It would not be a sensible move on his part after their last encounter, when the emotion had been so heightened between them he had had to walk away from it.

He had told himself to go to his own bedroom, and forget all about Brynne Sullivan. But his feet had seemed to have a different idea of his intentions as he had found himself knocking on her door!

It was there still, a tension, a frisson, that he could feel stretching across the room between them.

Even in pyjamas Brynne looked beautiful, her hair draped across one shoulder and down over her breasts. Firm, uptilting breasts, the nipples of which were outlined against the soft peach-coloured material of her top. Alejandro's lips tingled just at the thought of tasting the rosy tip with his tongue—

'If you are sure you are all right…' He nodded abruptly, knowing he had to leave now or put into practice all the things he was imagining doing with Brynne.

'Yes, of course I—' Brynne broke off, having started to cross the room to encourage his exit before coming to an abrupt halt, wincing slightly as she did so. 'I'm fine,' she told him brightly. 'Just fine.'

Alejandro's brow furrowed. 'Somehow I do not think so…' he murmured slowly, stepping farther into the bedroom.

'Please, Alejandro,' she said in protest, knowing that she shouldn't have moved, because it had caused the material of her top to rub painfully over her red and throbbing back. 'What could possibly be wrong?' she dismissed.

'I do not—' He broke off, standing only inches away from her now as he looked down into her face. 'You look—strained…' he finally murmured.

'Well, that's hardly flattering, Alejandro,' she told him dryly, wishing he would just leave.

She needed him to go now, and not just because she desperately needed to put some more cream on her back!

Alejandro shook his head, not in the least convinced by her attempt at humour. 'I refuse to leave until you tell me what is wrong, Brynne,' he said firmly.

She gave a disbelieving laugh. 'I could just scream,' she warned.

Her humour was still forced, in Alejandro's opinion. 'Is it Michael? Your parents, perhaps? Tell me what is wrong, Brynne,' he repeated sharply.

Her mouth set stubbornly. 'Nothing is—oh, very well,' she snapped impatiently as Alejandro continued to look at her. 'I just stayed out in the sun too long this afternoon, that's all. Are you satisfied? Will you leave my bedroom now?' She glared at him, colour flooding her cheeks.

It was what he should do, Alejandro knew. To do anything else could be dangerous in the extreme.

But he also knew that the Majorcan sun could be fierce in the afternoons, and if Brynne really had stayed out in it too long…

'Show me,' he said impatiently.

Brynne stared up at him with wide eyes. Show him? Take her top off and—

No way! There was absolutely no way she was going

to undress for this man, even though the idea was making her body tingle all over.

'I don't think so,' she told him primly. 'I'm quite capable of dealing with it myself, thank you,' she added defiantly as he still stood looking at her in that arrogant way that said he could be just as stubborn as she could.

'Obviously not if you are still in pain,' Alejandro rasped tersely.

'I've put some after-sun on,' she assured him irritably as she moved across the room to pick the bottle up from the bedside table. 'Here. See.' She held it up.

'On where?' His voice was silkily smooth.

She could feel the heat in her cheeks once again. 'On my back. Now would you please—'

'You cannot possibly reach the whole of your back,' Alejandro told her with maddening accuracy.

Brynne was becoming more and more agitated by the minute.

Wasn't it humiliating enough that he had kissed her earlier, that she had found herself becoming aroused just by his presence in this room, without having to bare her back to him?

'I can reach far enough,' she told him stubbornly.

'I disagree—'

'Do you know something, Alejandro?' she interrupted. 'It's of absolutely no interest to me whether or not you agree or disagree with me! Now please leave my bedroom before I start to scream with rage!'

Alejandro continued to look at her, noting the fire in her eyes, and the flush to her cheeks. But was that with temper? Or something else…?

He shrugged. 'Perhaps that is the answer, after all,'

he murmured as he took the bottle of after-sun from her unresisting fingers and began to unscrew the top. 'If Maria comes in answer to your scream then she can put on the after-sun for you instead of me!' he said in a mocking tone as Brynne frowned.

He was nowhere near as calm and controlled as he wished to appear though. The thought of running his hands across Brynne's back, and feeling her soft skin beneath his fingertips, was playing havoc with his self-control. His hands shook slightly as he tipped some of the after-sun lotion into the palm of his hand.

'Do as I say, Brynne,' he told her, his voice coming out harshly as he acknowledged his deepening arousal. And he hadn't even touched her yet!

Brynne glared at him for several more seconds before letting her breath out in an angry hiss. 'Oh, all right!' she snapped before marching over to the bed and lying down on her stomach, pulling the back of her top up as she did so. At least she could try to protect some of her modesty—

'That will not do, Brynne,' Alejandro said quietly from just behind her. 'I cannot reach your shoulders or the top of your back like that,' he explained patiently as she turned to frown at him.

No, he couldn't, could he? she conceded with an irritated sigh, sitting up to turn away from him as she undid the buttons to her top—mainly so that he shouldn't see the way her hands were shaking!

'Will you please look the other way for a moment?' she told him uncomfortably, waiting until he had done so before dropping her top to the floor and then quickly moving to lie face down on the bed once again, her face burning now rather than her back—with pure embarrassment!

Alejandro sat down on the side of the bed to rub some of the cream onto his hands, then began to caress the lotion into her burning shoulders, relieving some of the soreness but at the same time instantly creating a burning sensation somewhere else in her body.

Brynne's skin felt just as luxuriously silky as Alejandro had imagined it would, and his hands were necessarily gentle as he sensed her discomfort.

As he leant forward he could see the gentle swell of her breasts as they pressed into the cool sheets beneath her, a tantalizing glimpse that made him long to see them fully. He imagined running his hands over her there too, to bring her another sort of relief—

'To lie out in the sun and let yourself get burnt like this was an extremely stupid thing to do,' he declared harshly in an effort to hide his rapidly rising desire.

Brynne lifted her head to glare at him. 'Oh, yes, I just sat out there and got burnt on purpose!' she replied scathingly. 'I fell asleep, okay?' she added as she once again buried her face into the pillow.

Alejandro smiled slightly at her obvious annoyance with herself.

'I hope that isn't a smirk I see on your face, Alejandro Santiago!' Brynne said indignantly, having opened one eye to look at him.

His smile deepened. 'You sound like my mother when she used to chastise me as a child,' he explained as he could see Brynne's exasperation rising. 'Except she always used my full name of Alejandro Miguel Diego Santiago!'

'Perhaps I will too now that I know what it is!' Brynne muttered irritably—at the same time as she realized that one of his middle names was Miguel, the same as Michael.

Had Joanna known that when she had named their son, or was it just a coincidence?

Coincidence or not, it certainly served as a reminder of exactly who and what Alejandro was!

'I'm not sure that Señorina Roig would be too happy if she could see you right now,' she murmured tauntingly.

'Antonia?' She could feel Alejandro's hands tense at her mention of the other woman's name. 'What does Antonia have to do with my helping you deal with your sunburn?' he demanded haughtily.

'In my bedroom helping me deal with my sunburn,' Brynne corrected pointedly. 'In my bedroom helping me deal with my sunburn while I'm only half-dressed,' she added. 'She may just decide to call off the engagement if she knew.'

She felt the bed give slightly as Alejandro stood up abruptly, and Brynne reached out to pick up her top from the floor, holding it protectively against her as she sat up to face him.

To say he looked angry was an understatement. His eyes had turned pale silver, the arrogant planes of his face were enhanced by his tightly clenched jaw and his nostrils flared in the aquiline nose.

'There is no engagement,' he bit out icily. 'There will never be an engagement between myself and Antonia Roig.'

Alejandro was more furious than Brynne had ever seen him—although she had no idea why her teasing should have roused him so intensely…

She gave a shrug. 'Perhaps you haven't made that plain enough to Miss Roig yet, because I'm pretty sure that she was lining up boarding-schools in her head earlier for Michael once the two of you are married.'

Alejandro's eyes glittered coldly. 'You were mistaken,' he said tightly.

She had introduced the subject of Antonia as a means of putting an end to a situation that was becoming far too intimate for her comfort, but she hadn't expected it to succeed quite as well as it had.

She gave a puzzled frown. 'It was just an idea…'

'Once again it is an example of your interference in something that is none of your concern—'

'If she becomes Michael's stepmother it will be my concern—'

'She will not!' His accent was so thick now Brynne thought he was in danger of lapsing into his native tongue completely. 'Miguel will never have a stepmother, Antonia or any other woman, because I never intend to marry again! There, does that satisfy your curiosity?' he rasped harshly.

Again…

Alejandro had said he would never marry 'again'…?

CHAPTER SEVEN

He HAD said too much, Alejandro realized in disgust as the desire he had been feeling only minutes ago faded as if it had never been.

He had told Brynne Sullivan far too much.

Far more than she needed to know!

She was looking at him now with wide, suspicious eyes, as if the fact that he had once been married somehow made him into a—

'I married precisely three months after my brief relationship with Joanna was over,' he stated forcefully as he guessed the reason for the accusation in Brynne's gaze.

'That was convenient for you,' she replied hollowly, shaking her head slightly. 'No wonder you and Joanna never married—you were probably already married to someone else by the time she realized she was pregnant with Michael!'

'It was not like that at all—'

'Wasn't it?' Brynne scorned. 'Forgive me if I don't believe you!'

'I do not forgive you.' Alejandro was every inch the

wealthy, arrogant Spaniard as he looked down at her with icy grey eyes. 'Once again you speak of things, make accusations, you do not understand—'

'I understand you were married to someone else while Joanna had your baby, completely on her own!'

'I did not know she was pregnant—'

'And what would you have done about it if you had?' Brynne questioned. 'Paid for her to have an abortion? Or confessed all to your wife of only a few months and ruined her life as well? Although the fact that the two of you are no longer married probably shows that she at least had enough sense to leave you!' She was breathing hard in her agitation.

Alejandro had never received such insults to his honour before, from either a man or a woman, and the fact that minutes ago he had ached with wanting this particular woman only seemed to make it all the worse that the insults came from her.

His mouth twisted. 'My wife is dead. And there would have been no question of Joanna having an abortion! If Joanna had told me of her pregnancy, I would have supported both her and my child.'

'It must be nice to be rich enough to be able to salvage your conscience so easily!' Brynne scorned.

'If you were a man I would have knocked you down for the insults you have given me tonight,' Alejandro bit out coldly. 'But as you are not, I instead think it best that I leave you now to give you chance to calm down. We can talk about this again in the morning if that is what you wish.'

What she wished was that she had never met him—and her reasons for that no longer concerned Michael alone!

Minutes ago she had known herself aroused by Alejandro. And not for the first time, either.

What she really wanted to do right now was sit down and have a good cry at her own stupidity in allowing herself to become attracted to this complicated man!

She could so easily have turned over on the bed a few minutes ago and pulled his head down to hers and have him kiss her until she could think of nothing and no one but him. She longed to have him caress her in all the places that ached for his touch.

She was as disturbed by that admission as she was by learning he had been married.

'I don't know what I'll want in the morning,' she said dully.

But she did know. She wanted to go home, back to England, to forget she had ever met this unfathomable man. And instead she had to stay on here, for Michael's sake…

'Please go now,' she told Alejandro flatly.

Alejandro looked at her bowed head, and the beautiful hair that cascaded over the bareness of her delicate shoulders like a living flame. As he stared at her endearing freckles he had longed to kiss such a short time ago some of the anger he was feeling left him.

He had not thought it necessary for Brynne to know the details of his relationship with Joanna or the circumstances of his marriage to Francesca, and, knowing how close he had come tonight to taking her in his arms and making love to her, he believed that more than ever.

Brynne Sullivan was the last woman he should ever make love to!

'Perhaps you are right,' he snapped.

'Yes.' She sighed, reaching up a hand to push back the thickness of her hair to look up at him with pained blue eyes.

Alejandro looked at her for several more seconds before turning sharply on his heel and walking to the door, closing it softly behind him as he left.

He closed his eyes as he leant back against the wall outside in the hallway, fighting the yearning he had to go back into the room, to take Brynne into his arms.

But he had made a decision when Francesca had died five years ago that any relationship he had in future would only ever be of the transient kind, of short duration, with no emotional entanglement, and Brynne Sullivan, he already knew, with her prim morality, and her soul-destroying blue eyes, was not a woman of that type.

Brynne felt gritty-eyed and irritable from lack of sleep the next morning. She'd found it hard to sleep after the things she had learnt about Alejandro.

He had probably been engaged when he and Joanna had met seven years ago and already married by the time Joanna had known she was expecting his baby. Although it appeared that his wife had died some time in the last seven years.

All of these things had gone round and round in her head for hours last night.

One thing she did know was that any growing attraction she might have felt towards Alejandro had to stop.

It should never have happened in the first place after the battle the two of them had had six weeks ago over the custody of Michael!

In fact, the more she came to know about Alejandro Santiago, the stronger her feeling that Michael should have been allowed to stay with her.

The fact that Alejandro was sitting alone at the dining table, calmly reading a newspaper, when she got downstairs for breakfast did nothing to improve her mood!

Alejandro looked up as he sensed Brynne quietly entering the room, his mouth tightening as she avoided meeting his gaze to go over to the side dresser and pour herself some juice.

'Where's Michael?' she asked as she came to sit at the table opposite him.

'He went down to the orchard with Maria to pick some fresh oranges,' Alejandro dismissed, carefully folding his newspaper to place it on the table beside him. 'Is juice all you are having for breakfast?' He frowned.

Brynne shrugged dismissively. 'I'm not hungry.'

'How are you feeling this morning?' he probed softly.

She raised her chin, her blue eyes bright with challenge. 'How should I be feeling?'

He shrugged his broad shoulders. 'I merely wondered if your back was still painful…?'

'Oh.' Her gaze once again avoided his. 'It's much better this morning, thank you.'

She didn't look better, Alejandro noted, seeing that her face was pale and that there were dark shadows beneath her eyes.

He nodded abruptly. 'That is good. I have some business to attend to in Palma today,' he said curtly. 'Will you and Michael be able to amuse yourselves by the pool? With the appropriately applied suntan lotion, of course,' he added ruefully.

'Of course,' Brynne echoed dryly. 'If Michael gets bored I can always take him for a walk to Banyalbufar. Maria says its only just up the coast and—'

'I would rather you did not walk anywhere today,' Alejandro cut in.

'I'm sure the walk will do Raul and Rafael good,' Brynne finished mockingly. 'From their unhealthy pallor they obviously don't get out in the sun enough!'

'But you have,' Alejandro spoke firmly. 'And to go out walking when you are already burnt is not wise.'

Brynne gave him a scathing glance. 'I think I'm old enough to know not to make the same mistake twice!'

Alejandro gave her a searching look. Were they still talking about yesterday's sunburn? Or something else…?

From her guarded response to his earlier enquiry as to how she was feeling this morning he would say it was something else!

Her skin had felt wonderful to the touch last night as he had carefully applied the soothing lotion to her shoulders and the curve of her spine, and he was experienced enough to know that Brynne had enjoyed the caress of his hands. But if she feared he would suggest repeating the process then she was mistaken.

He had paid for his own unsatisfied arousal with a sleepless night, and did not intend repeating the experience!

'I suggest you ask Maria to put some after-sun on your back before you go outside,' he snapped dismissively, throwing his napkin down on the table to stand up. 'I am not sure what time I will get back, so do not—'

'Oh, please don't hurry back on our account,' Brynne assured him derisively, relieved to know that he would probably be out most of the day. 'Michael and I are quite used to entertaining ourselves.'

Alejandro looked down at her coldly before turning on his heel and striding from the room.

Brynne heaved a deep sigh of relief as she relaxed the tension from her shoulders. Painful shoulders, as it happened, with the skin on her back bright red this morning and slightly itchy. No doubt it would start to peel in a couple of days, and then instead of having the appearance of a lobster she would look like a snake shedding its skin. Very attractive!

Although if Alejandro was looking for attractive, he didn't have to look any further than Antonia Roig!

A fact Brynne was made very aware of later that morning when a red sports car roared down the driveway with Antonia sitting behind the wheel as she parked the car beside the villa with an assurance that spoke of familiarity.

Brynne's heart sank as she watched the other woman run her hands through her tumbled dark curls and replenish the red gloss to her lips before sliding out from behind the wheel; the white sundress she wore suiting her smoothly olive complexion and emphasizing the voluptuous curves of her body.

In contrast, Brynne felt at a complete disadvantage, having pulled on a loose white shirt over her bikini after taking a dip with Michael in the pool, her wet hair now slicked back from a face completely bare of make-up.

She stood up as Antonia walked over gracefully on white, high-heeled, designer mules. 'I'm afraid Alejandro isn't here at the moment, Miss Roig,' she began politely.

The other woman gave a gracious inclination of her head. 'He is in Palma today.'

If Alejandro had already told Antonia that, then what was she doing here…?

'Can I offer you some refreshment?' Brynne indicated the jug of fresh orange juice Maria had brought out minutes ago for her and Michael to enjoy, not particularly wanting the other woman to stay any longer than she had to, but at the same time realizing Antonia had other ideas.

'That would be acceptable.' Antonia nodded before sitting down on the lounger next to Brynne's, her eyes hidden behind dark sunglasses as she glanced over to where Michael was throwing euro coins to the bottom of the pool before diving down to collect them. 'He is so like Alejandro, is he not.' It was a statement rather than a question.

'Yes.' What else could Brynne say? The likeness between father and son was indisputable.

'Thank you,' Antonia said as she accepted the glass of juice before placing it down on the table untouched, her long nails still tipped in the red that matched her lipgloss. 'Miguel is the son of your sister…?' she prompted without so much as a polite preliminary.

Brynne's wariness grew at this unexpected visit by the other woman. 'My sister-in-law, actually,' she said.

'Your sister-in-law…?'

Brynne nodded. 'It's a little complicated, but, yes, Joanna was my sister-in-law.'

Anotnia's pouting red lips tightened slightly. 'Alejandro is very anxious that Miguel should…adapt…to his new way of life as quickly as possible,' she declared, obviously deciding not to pursue the subject of Brynne's specific relationship to Michael.

Brynne was starting to like this conversation less and less!

'Yes,' she answered noncommittally.

Antonia gave a shrug of her smoothly bare shoulders. 'As such it would probably be better for Miguel if he were to spend more time with—people of his own kind.'

Meaning what, precisely? Brynne wondered guardedly. Did Antonia mean the people of Majorca and Spain? Or did she mean affluently rich people like her and her father, and Alejandro himself, of course? Something Brynne obviously wasn't!

'Alejandro hasn't said that,' she replied truthfully. He had made it clear he didn't want her here, but not for that reason.

'Alejandro is very much the *caballero*, you know,' Antonia told her with an indulgent smile. 'Always the gentleman,' she explained for Brynne's benefit.

Brynne knew what a '*caballero*' was—she just didn't particularly associate Alejandro with one!

Although perhaps that was being a little unfair. Alejandro was always aware of the social niceties expected of him, was unfailingly polite to his employees, receiving their loyalty, and possibly their affection, in return. It was only with Brynne that he seemed to have trouble maintaining that politeness!

And she certainly didn't appreciate this woman's implication that Brynne had to be aware she wasn't wanted here. Or the fact that Alejandro obviously had to have discussed that subject with Antonia for the other woman to know that!

'I'm sure that if Alejandro wishes to…change our arrangement…he will tell me so,' she told Antonia stiffly, knowing that Alejandro had told her from the start that he didn't want her here, but that she had chosen to ignore it. Obviously by talking to Antonia on the subject he had decided to bring in reinforcements!

'That is a little…difficult…in the circumstances, is it not?' the other woman pointed out. 'Besides, it is so much more…civilized…for the women to talk of these things, yes?' she added sweetly.

Brynne's dislike of this beautiful but venomous woman was growing by the moment. As was her anger towards Alejandro for having discussed this situation with the woman who appeared to be his mistress even if he didn't intend her to be his wife.

'I'm sorry, Miss Roig. I appreciate that you and Alejandro are—friends,' she bit out tensely as she stood up, 'but I really have no intention of discussing something so—so personal, with someone I hardly know.' She glared down at the other woman pointedly as she willed her to leave.

Antonia stood up slowly, completely unruffled as she smoothed the white sundress down over shapely legs. 'I was merely trying to be—kind, Miss Sullivan,' she soothed huskily, smiling slightly. 'As I said earlier, Alejandro is too much the gentleman to be quite so… frank…with you.'

Brynne gave a scornful smile. 'That hasn't been my experience so far!' she dismissed impatiently. 'Now, if you wouldn't mind? Michael and I are going for a walk this morning.'

The other woman gave her a considering look. 'You

must be careful of too much sun, Miss Sullivan,' she advised lightly. 'A golden tan is acceptable, but with your fair colouring you are sure to burn.'

Exactly when had Alejandro spoken to this woman about her? After he had left her bedroom last night? Or had it been first thing this morning?

Well, if he thought telling his girlfriend to come and have a little 'woman to woman' chat with her was going to persuade Brynne into leaving here, then he was going to be sadly disappointed.

It was more likely to have the opposite effect!

CHAPTER EIGHT

'How dare you ask that—that—woman to come here and tell me you want me to leave?'

Alejandro had spent a long day in Palma, locked in further negotiations with Felipe Roig, tired of the cat-and-mouse game Felipe seemed to be having with him as he gave the older man the warning that he might withdraw from the possible deal himself if it wasn't soon settled to his satisfaction. A warning Felipe had obviously taken seriously enough to waste a day of Alejandro's time!

Alejandro would rather have come home once it had become obvious that no deal would be reached today, but the older man had insisted that the two of them had to go out to an early dinner in order to show that they were still friends. As Alejandro still had every intention of buying the tract of land Felipe had for sale, he didn't intend being anything else until he had Felipe's signature on a contract.

But having finally returned to the villa at nine-thirty that evening, he had gone to the pool-house to change into black swimming trunks before diving straight into

the refreshing water and swimming half a dozen lengths
of the pool before he had felt his temper start to cool.
Another argument with Brynne was the last thing he felt
in the mood for…

He rested his arms on the edge of the pool as he
looked up at her, taking a few seconds to appreciate how
sexily attractive she looked in the sky-blue linen dress
with her feet bare beneath tanned legs. Her hair was
loose about her shoulders and her face beautiful in spite
of the angry glitter he could see in her eyes and that
becoming flush to her cheeks.

It was an angry beauty he was becoming all too used
to where this particular woman was concerned!

'I have no idea what you are talking about, Brynne—
and, quite frankly, at this moment I do not think I want
to know.' He sighed, holding up a silencing hand. 'I am
tired and dusty from my frustrating day in Palma, so if
you can wait a few minutes before continuing this tirade,
then I would like a glass of cool wine first…' He levered
himself quickly out of the water.

Brynne's breath instantly caught in her throat at the
sight of all that bare male beauty. Alejandro's skin was
dark olive all over, his legs long, his shoulders broad,
chest muscled, stomach flat…

She averted her gaze but couldn't resist looking back
again as Alejandro strolled over to the pool bar to take
a cooled bottle of wine from the refrigerator there,
deftly removing the cork before placing two glasses on
top of the bar.

God, he really was the most gorgeous—

'Would you like some?' He held up the bottle invitingly.

Why not? She wasn't tired and dusty, but she could

definitely do with something to soothe her frayed nerves. Waiting for Alejandro to come back to the villa had been tediously long, and on top of that her irritation had grown when he hadn't got back in time to say goodnight to Michael, but she'd had no intention of going to bed herself until after she had spoken to him.

Finding herself in the company of an almost naked Alejandro—those black swimming trunks resting low on lean hips almost didn't count!—was making her senses dance with an altogether different emotion, the dark hair slicked back from those arrogantly handsome features making her mouth go dry.

'Thank you,' she accepted stiltedly as she took the glass of wine he held out to her. 'You—'

'At least let me have one drink before you start again!' Alejandro drawled as he sat down tiredly on one of the loungers, unconcerned by the wetness of his hair and body as he took several sips of the wine before looking up at her enquiringly. 'You may now continue,' he invited mockingly.

Brynne gave him a quelling glance. 'I'm glad you find all of this funny, Alejandro,' she dismissed in disgust, desperately trying to rekindle her earlier anger, but finding it increasing difficult in the company of this compellingly handsome man.

Come on, Brynne, she chided herself impatiently. Alejandro wasn't the first man she had seen in a pair of bathing trunks.

No…but he was the first one to make her want to rip that last remaining garment from that leanly muscled frame so that she could gaze her fill of all of him.

She shook her head in disbelief. 'I, on the other

hand,' she snapped waspishly, 'as the recipient of this "woman-to-woman" so-called advice, don't find any of this in the least funny.'

No, she obviously didn't find it funny, Alejandro acknowledged as he saw that the shadows beneath her eyes had deepened since this morning, her mouth curved down unhappily. Whatever it was!

'Perhaps you are not explaining yourself very well.' He smiled ruefully, leaning back against the cushioned chair and taking another sip of his wine.

The swim had been so cool, so reviving, the wine even more so; after hours of fruitless discussion his throat had felt rough as well as dry.

It was also, he realized, frowning, good to come home and find a beautiful woman waiting for him...

'No—you aren't listening!' Brynne paced restlessly beside the pool on those surprisingly pretty feet. 'And would it have been too much trouble for you to have come home in time to say goodnight to Michael?'

Alejandro closed his eyes briefly before looking up at her. This woman still dared to meddle in things he would accept from no one else. 'I do have a business to run—'

'And was your business any more successful today?' she challenged scathingly.

'As it happens, no.' Alejandro sat forward to replenish his wineglass, his relaxation of a few minutes ago fading as rapidly as the sun now disappearing beneath the horizon. 'Felipe continues to be...elusive...concerning finalizing the deal.' His expression was grim.

'Then perhaps you should become the elusive one,' Brynne dismissed, aware that they were once again veering off the subject—and the more time she spent in

Alejandro's almost-naked company, the less angry and more tinglingly aware of him she was becoming.

Alejandro raised dark brows. 'I beg your pardon?'

Brynne gave a shrug. 'That's the way it usually works with my more disinterested students. The more I ignore them, the more they want me to take notice of them,' she explained at Alejandro's questioning look.

Alejandro continued to look puzzled for several moments, and then he gave a slight smile. 'And do you shout at these students in the way that you shout at me?'

Had she shouted at him? Probably, she realized with a wince.

After all, she had been waiting hours for him to come home, and the first awareness she had had of his arrival had been the sound of him swimming, without any concern, up and down the pool. Not a move that would soothe her temper!

She grimaced. 'No, I don't shout at them.'

Alejandro quirked dark brows. 'Only at me?'

Well…yes.

Despite her red hair, she didn't usually lose her temper with anyone; she was normally cheerfully calm. To shout at one of her students, at anyone, really, was to lose control of the situation, she had always thought.

Unfortunately she had lost control of the situation with Alejandro Santiago from the moment the judge had come down in his favour regarding custody of Michael.

She gave him a frustrated glance. 'You annoy me, yes—'

'And is that all I do to you, Brynne?' he interrupted huskily, putting down his wineglass to get slowly to his feet.

Her eyes widened in alarm as he padded softly towards her. Like a predatory animal approaching its prey, she realized as her pulse started to race.

Alejandro stopped only inches away from where she stood rooted to the spot, not touching her—not needing to...

The sheer height and breadth of him as he stood so close to her blocked out everything but the sight and warmth of him.

'Is it, Brynne?' he encouraged throatily.

She swallowed hard. 'I don't know what you mean.'

'Oh, yes,' he breathed, 'I think you know only too well.'

She could smell the all-male scent of him, making her long to touch him, to caress the hard strength of his shoulders, featherlight across his chest and down that flat, hard stomach. She wanted to reach out and pull his head down to hers even as he moulded her body against his, wanted—needed—to feel the hardness of him against her, to touch and be touched, to—

'You feel it too, do you not?' he murmured huskily.

'Feel what...?' she asked weakly.

But she knew. She knew!

'Did you know...' Alejandro spoke softly, one hand moving up to cup beneath her chin as he tilted her face up to his and looked deeply into her eyes. 'Did you know,' he murmured again, that silver gaze holding her captive, his lips only centimetres away from hers now, 'that you have extremely beautiful feet?'

It was so not what Brynne had been expecting to hear, the very air between them so tense with expectation, that for a moment she could only look up at him blankly.

And then she blinked, once, twice, a frown appearing between dark blue eyes. 'I have beautiful feet…?' she finally repeated huskily with a hint of incredulity.

'You do.' Alejandro breathed softly even as his lips took slow possession of hers.

Brynne swayed weakly against him, her hands at last moving up to those oh-so-strong shoulders, finding them just as muscled and yet warmly sensual to the touch as she had imagined they would be. She groaned low in her throat as Alejandro's tongue parted her lips to deepen the kiss, his hands splayed against her spine as he drew her close against him.

Brynne felt the force of his arousal against her stomach as the kiss became more intense, more intimate. Alejandro's mouth became fierce against hers, the thrust of his tongue creating an answering warmth between her thighs, a heat that was both moist and urgent.

She clung to his shoulders as, his mouth still plundering hers, Alejandro lifted her up in his arms and carried her over to lay her down on the sun-warmed grass, her arms moving up about his shoulders as he lay down beside her.

He lifted his head to look down at her, the last of the sun's red rays turning her hair to fire against the green of the grass, her eyes darkly blue, her mouth poutingly aroused from his kisses.

His gaze was caught and held by those full lips as he bent his head to draw her lower lip into the heat of his mouth, sucking gently, groaning low in his throat as he felt the quivers of pleasure down the slender length of her body.

Touching and kissing Brynne Sullivan was something he wanted badly, something he had been wanting for a long time.

But, like yesterday, kissing wasn't enough. He wanted more.

His lifted his head, easily holding her gaze with his as he moved one of his hands to undo the buttons down the front of her dress. He smoothed the material aside to reveal completely unrestrained breasts, shifting his gaze to look at those pert, beautiful orbs, the nipples already roused and begging to be kissed.

Brynne gasped, her body arching as she felt the first touch of Alejandro's lips against her bared breasts, his tongue tasting, teeth gently rasping, before he drew that heated tip into the warm cavern of his mouth, suckling, first gently, then harder.

She couldn't think, couldn't see, couldn't feel anything but Alejandro and the pleasure he was giving as his hand moved as surely to her other breast, the pad of his thumb moving there with the same rhythm as his lips sucked and his tongue rasped so erotically.

She moved her hips restlessly against him as she felt her need grow, wanting, aching for, some sort of release from this burning need that was threatening to tear her apart.

Alejandro was suddenly above her, their bodies moulded together from breast to thigh. The movement of his thighs against hers told her of his own pulsing arousal as he looked down at her with fierce silver eyes.

'Tell me what you want, Brynne,' he encouraged gruffly.

'Alejandro—'

'Tell me, Brynne.' he repeated fiercely before his

head lowered, his gaze holding hers as his tongue rasped erotically across her already sensitized nipple.

Brynne trembled even as she arched against him, her hand moving up instinctively as she held his head against her.

It was all the encouragement Alejandro needed. He suckled fiercely, teeth gently biting, tongue caressing, a flush to his cheeks minutes later when he raised his head to look at her. 'Do you want me to make love to you, Brynne?' he prompted forcefully.

Yes…

She had never wanted anything as badly as she wanted Alejandro at that moment, her nails digging into his shoulders, her heart beating so loudly she was sure he must be able to hear it.

She moistened her lips, her breath shallow in her chest as she felt herself held captive by that compelling gaze. 'I—'

'Shh!' He became suddenly still beside her, raising his head, more like the hunter this time than the predator as he tilted his head to listen, eyes narrowing. 'I hear a car.' He rolled onto the grass beside her, his hands moving to the folds of her dress, pulling them back over her nakedness.

He heard a car?

Brynne hadn't been aware of anything but Alejandro, of the touch of his hands, the caress of his lips and tongue, totally lost to the sensuality of the moment, her whole body trembling with the anticipation of this man's possession.

Unlike Alejandro, who heard a car!

CHAPTER NINE

'Who—?'

'The who does not matter,' Alejandro rasped as he stood up impatiently, very aware now of the rapidly approaching car.

And unsure of whether to be annoyed or relieved at the interruption!

Making love to Brynne Sullivan, much as he might have wanted it, was not a good idea. In fact, it was more recklessly stupid than anything he had ever done before!

More stupid than his relationship with Joanna all those years ago.

More stupid than his marriage to a woman he had not loved and who most certainly had not loved him.

His eyes were cold now as he looked down at a still-dazed Brynne, running a hand through the damp length of his hair as he heard the car stopping at the back of the villa. 'As we are about to have company I suggest you cover yourself,' he snapped.

Brynne's shock was starting to fade now, the cool night air on her damp flesh probably contributing to that, she acknowledged self-disgustedly even as she began to do up the buttons on her dress with slightly trembling fingers.

What had happened just now?

What had she allowed to happen?

One minute she and Alejandro had been arguing as they usually did, and the next—

She closed her eyes in embarrassment as she remembered what had happened next!

How on earth had she allowed things to go as far as they had?

Because she had wanted Alejandro with a madness that had driven everything else from her mind and body, had been wanton in his arms, her body still trembling with that need, her breasts still aching, the throbbing warmth between her thighs telling her how near she had come to losing control completely.

God, what must Alejandro think of her?

She didn't even want to think about that now, couldn't think about it, daren't think about it…!

But as she heard the familiar click of high heels on the villa's tiled pathway she knew that the 'who' did matter, after all, sure that their visitor, Alejandro's visitor, was going to be none other than the beautiful Antonia Roig!

Brynne rose quickly to her feet, standing several feet away from Alejandro as Antonia came through the arched gateway at the side of the villa, as sexily alluring as usual in a black fitted dress that left her shoulders bare, its knee-length also revealing her shapely legs.

Was this meeting prearranged? Brynne wondered. Or was Alejandro as surprised at the woman's visit as she was?

His greeting was warm enough as he strolled across to meet the other woman. 'Antonia,' he murmured huskily as he bent to kiss her on both cheeks.

Brynne turned away as she saw the beautiful Antonia reach up to complete the affectionate gesture by placing her red-painted lips against his in the third kiss that confirmed their intimacy with each other.

She had to get away from here.

Now!

Alejandro frowned darkly, slightly annoyed with Antonia for turning up uninvited in this way, but at the same time knowing he should probably be grateful for the interruption, because she had prevented him from making a serious mistake where Brynne Sullivan was concerned.

He was normally a cautious man when it came to his involvement with women, but Brynne had somehow managed to slip beneath his guard, making him forget, however briefly, all of the reasons he had told himself he should not pursue the sexual awareness he had sensed was growing between the two of them.

An awareness he now needed to dispel as quickly as possible!

'How kind of you to come and share your evening with me.' He smiled at Antonia. 'Would you care for a glass of wine?' he invited as they turned.

He couldn't help but notice Antonia's start of surprise as she saw Brynne standing a short distance away—her dress thankfully rebuttoned, although her glorious hair did look slightly wilder than normal.

Antonia's eyes narrowed briefly, losing some of their warmth, before she collected herself enough to resume smiling. 'Miss Sullivan,' she greeted lightly. 'How lovely to see you again,' she added almost questioningly.

'Señorita Roig,' Brynne came back stiffly. 'If you will both excuse me?' she added abruptly, head bent as she moved swiftly towards the villa.

It was what Alejandro had wanted, needing time away from Brynne to collect his scattered wits. For surely they had to have left him for him to have been so reckless as to kiss and touch her in the way that he had?

But as he saw the pallor of Brynne's cheeks, the slight trembling of her lips, the telling glitter to those dark blue eyes, he felt a moment's regret for deliberately hurting her in this way.

'Brynne!' he called after her sharply.

She stopped hesitantly, that tear-wet gaze not quite meeting his as she turned back slightly. 'Yes…?'

'Will you excuse me a moment, Antonia?' He turned back briefly to the woman at his side. 'I—have something I need to tell Brynne before she retires for the evening.' His smile was warmly placating.

'I understand, Alejandro.' Antonia gazed up at him warmly, mouth full and pouting. 'Do not be away too long, hmm?' she added with sensuous invitation as long red-tipped fingers ran caressingly down his cheek.

Brynne watched the intimate exchange between Alejandro and Antonia with mounting humiliation.

She had forgotten, as Alejandro had kissed her, that the reason she had waited so impatiently for his return this evening was because she had wanted to complain of the things this woman had said to her earlier today.

Now, witnessing that warm familiarity between the two of them, the look of triumph in Antonia's gaze as she glanced across at her so dismissively, Brynne thought it too late to make those complaints!

'What do you want, Alejandro?' she muttered impatiently as he reached her side.

His face tightened at her dismissive tone. 'You were the one who wanted to talk to me about something earlier…?' he reminded curtly.

Brynne could have laughed at the ridiculousness of talking about that now; Antonia Roig, despite Alejandro's denials to the contrary, obviously had her red-tipped claws into him so deeply he was unlikely to disapprove of anything the other woman said or did, but especially to Brynne, whom he considered an unwelcome guest in his home, at best.

'It doesn't matter.' She sighed.

His gaze narrowed. 'It mattered enough earlier for you to verbally berate me in the way that you did.'

Brynne gave a humourless laugh. 'I'm always "verbally berating" you, Alejandro—or hadn't you noticed?'

Oh, he had noticed. It was one of the things that made Brynne so different from every other woman he had ever known; none of them, including his wife, Francesca, had ever dared to talk to him in the way that Brynne did.

'Please go back to Miss Roig,' Brynne added with abrupt dismissal. 'I'm sure that she will be only too pleased to…soothe you, after your troubled day!' she added scathingly, that blue gaze raised in challenge to his.

Alejandro regretted even more having deliberately hurt Brynne, after their closeness of earlier, with his implied intimacy of a relationship with Antonia. But he also knew that it was for the best. He had nothing to offer a woman like Brynne—not love, and certainly not permanence.

'I am sure that she will too,' he replied mockingly. 'Goodnight, Brynne,' he added with cool dismissal, turning away to walk back to where Antonia waited for him.

Brynne turned sharply on her heel as she saw Antonia turn to Alejandro, murmuring something softly to him before the two of them laughed companionably.

At her, probably!

Or was she just being paranoid? Oversensitive from her time spent in Alejandro's arms?

Probably, she accepted heavily as she went slowly up the stairs. Alejandro might be many things—fickle obviously being one of them!—but she very much doubted that he was a man who discussed his conquests, especially with a woman who was another one of them.

But at least Antonia's arrival had stopped her making a complete idiot of herself, Brynne acknowledged with clenched jaw and gritted teeth as she heard the other woman's husky laugh several more times as she sat up in her bedroom once again trying to interest herself in the book she had brought away with her.

Again a useless exercise, when her thoughts were tormented with visions of what Alejandro and Antonia would be doing together when the laughter stopped!

She threw the book down on the bed and stood up, deliberately not approaching the window as she paced the room restlessly, having no intention of letting either Alejandro or Antonia think she was actually spying on them.

God, she could do with a plunge into the pool herself, so hot were her memories of her time in Alejandro's arms!

Several of her boyfriends had lasted longer than a couple of dates, but with none of them had she ever felt that mindless need to know their possession, to just forget everything but the moment, to find a release that she had never known.

To still ache, hours later, for that fulfilment!

Her nerves jangled irritably as she once again heard Antonia's husky laughter. She threw herself down on the bed to pull one of the pillows over her head to shut out the sound.

She would get over this ridiculous fascination she seemed to have developed for Alejandro.

She would!

'What do you intend doing today?' Alejandro prompted politely as Brynne joined him at the breakfast table the following morning, his manner deliberately that of a host to a guest.

He had a need, after seriously stepping over a line the evening before, to establish their relationship back to one of formality.

Although Brynne looked less approachable herself this morning as she looked across at him coolly, the white cotton blouse and linen trousers she wore suiting her slenderness, her red hair secured loosely on top of her head.

'You really don't need to even pretend a polite interest in what I'm doing, you know, Alejandro,' she dismissed with a derisive laugh. 'We both know I'm only here on sufferance!'

Alejandro frowned his irritation at Brynne's tone—

that irritation at complete variance with his earlier decision to instigate a distance between them. 'As you are Miguel's aunt, I of course owe you a debt of gratitude for the way in which—'

'Michael's aunt through marriage,' Brynne corrected pointedly as she carefully replaced her coffee cup in the saucer. 'And as anything I may or may not have done for Michael was done out of love for him, I'm sure you know what you can do with your gratitude!' she added forcefully.

Alejandro had let her know quite clearly the night before that he regretted whatever lapse had induced him to make love to her—a lapse that Brynne probably regretted more than he did! He didn't have to treat her like some polite stranger this morning in order to emphasize that point!

He frowned darkly. 'I was merely—'

'I'm really not interested, Alejandro,' Brynne snapped irritably, pushing back her chair with the intention of standing up, but prevented from doing so as Alejandro reached out and grasped her hand. She trembled slightly. 'What are you doing?' She sighed her exasperation with this man's hot-and-cold moods.

He had no idea, Alejandro acknowledged with inward impatience for his own actions; he only felt a need to stop Brynne from leaving with things so strained between them.

He removed his hand, resting his elbows on the table as he steepled his fingers together. 'You wanted to say something to me last night...' he reminded huskily.

Brynne gave him a scathing glance. 'I'm sure that Antonia was only too eager, once I had gone to bed, to tell you all about our little chat yesterday morning!'

Antonia…? What did Antonia have to do with what had been troubling Brynne when he had arrived home yesterday evening?

What was it Brynne had said—attacked him with—last night? Something about that woman telling her he wanted her to leave, he recalled frowningly. He had been too tired and irritable at the time to consider Brynne's anger as anything more than yet another misunderstanding between them. But her mention of Antonia put an altogether different connotation on things.

Antonia had been the woman Brynne referred to…?

Alejandro's gaze became guarded as he looked across at a Brynne, who was obviously angry once again, a flush to her cheeks, her eyes sparkling with the emotion. 'Perhaps I would rather hear it from you…?' he said slowly.

'Well, that's just too bad!' she told him scathingly, standing up to look down at him. 'Because I have no intention of satisfying your curiosity! Suffice to say, I am not leaving here before my month is up, and nothing you can say, or do—or that your girlfriend says or does!—is going to make me leave any sooner. Is that clear enough for you?' she challenged.

'Very clear,' he acknowledged distractedly.

Antonia had come here yesterday while he was out? While she had known he was out in Palma at a meeting with her father?

Exactly what had she said to Brynne…?

Whatever it was he deeply resented Antonia thinking she had the right to come here when he was out and say anything at all of a personal nature to Brynne.

Yes, he had used Antonia's unexpected arrival yesterday evening as a means of ending that tense situation between himself and Brynne, which might or might not have given Antonia completely the wrong idea about their own relationship, but her conversation with Brynne had taken place before that…

'Perhaps you misunderstood Antonia? Her English was perhaps not as fluent—'

'Yes, you would like me to think that, wouldn't you?' Brynne scorned as she gave a rueful shake of her head. 'It hardly fits in with her claim of you "always being the gentleman", does it, to ask your mistress to come here and tell me it would be a good idea if I left?'

Alejandro's expression darkened even more. 'Antonia is not my mistress,' he bit out coldly. 'And I did not ask her to speak to you on this subject—'

'Of course you didn't,' Brynne dismissed wearily.

'Or any other,' Alejandro finished firmly, throwing his napkin down on the table before standing up, tall and forbidding in a black tee shirt and black denims. 'You will forget this conversation with Antonia ever happened,' he instructed arrogantly. 'I will speak to her—'

'In bed or out of it?' Brynne taunted, her anger of yesterday increased by the humiliation she had suffered after being in this man's arms last night.

Alejandro looked every inch the arrogant Spaniard at that moment, his eyes cold, his mouth a thin, angry line. 'You will forget the things Antonia has said to you,' he repeated icily. 'As I will do my best to forget that you have once again insulted my honour with your accusations—'

'Oh, please, Alejandro.' Brynne gave another weary sigh. 'This display of injured Spanish pride may work on some people, but it doesn't work on me!'

Alejandro wanted to make her listen to him. To take hold of her and shake her until her teeth rattled. To take her in his arms and kiss her until she was senselessly compliant…!

He forced himself to do none of those things, instead clenching his hands into fists at his sides. 'Nevertheless, I will ensure that Antonia does not talk to you in this way again,' he assured Brynne coldly. 'And I apologize on her behalf for any misunderstanding that may have arisen between the two of you,' he added stiffly.

'There was no misunderstanding,' Brynne assured him with a derisive shake of her head. 'And I'm sure she wouldn't thank you for implying that there was!'

His mouth tightened. He did not care whether Antonia thanked him or not. He allowed no one, absolutely no one, to act on his behalf in the way that Brynne claimed Antonia Roig had done yesterday.

'I am taking Miguel out with me today,' he informed Brynne distantly. 'Perhaps you would care to get his bathing things together while I ask Maria to pack a picnic lunch for the two of us? You may, if you wish, use one of the cars in the garage to go for the drive you were so keen to go on yesterday,' he added dismissively.

No suggestion of her accompanying the two of them, Brynne noted painfully, knowing that her hurt feelings on being excluded from the outing weren't in the least logical after her comments to Alejandro yesterday about not spending time with his young son, but feeling slightly put out anyway.

Michael, she knew, was still a little nervous of the man who was his father, and would still have welcomed her presence on any outing, so it had to be Alejandro who didn't want her with them...

Not surprisingly, really, she accepted heavily; the two of them were never exactly harmonious when they were together, were they?

Alejandro paused in the doorway. 'I think it best if you put Antonia's comments behind you, Brynne,' he bit out abruptly. 'It is finished. Over,' he assured her before turning sharply on his heel to stride forcefully from the dining-room.

Brynne gazed after him with a frown.

When he said, 'It is finished. Over,' did he mean his relationship with Antonia Roig, or just the other woman's interference in his personal affairs?

And wasn't that yet another thing that Alejandro would consider none of her business...?

CHAPTER TEN

MORE out of defiance than any real wish to go out on her own, Brynne did go for a drive once Michael and Alejandro had gone out in the Mercedes, selecting a car with a soft top she could put down to enjoy the full benefits of the beautifully sunny day.

Whether out of defiance or not, she actually enjoyed her day out, driving down to Palma to park on the seafront and walk along the marina looking at the magnificent yachts moored there, some of them looking bigger inside than the flat she rented at home, and several of them had helicopter pads on the back too.

She bought a baguette for her lunch, finding a park just across from the seafront in which to sit and enjoy it along with lots of other tourists sitting or lying about the wonderful water feature in the park's middle, and then strolling into the city to sit outside a café and have a leisurely cup of coffee before wandering up to look at the cathedral.

Michael, as a six-year-old, would have enjoyed looking at the yachts for a short time, but the cathedral wouldn't have interested him in the slightest, so it felt quite good to take full advantage of this day off.

But lonely too, of course…

And she couldn't help wondering where Alejandro had taken his son for the day, sincerely hoped, for both their sakes, that Alejandro had taken Michael's age into account when he had made his plans.

Not that it was any of her business, of course, but she was aware of the time passing, and would feel happier herself knowing that Michael was going to be happy once she had returned home.

She returned to the villa shortly after five o'clock to find they had only just returned themselves. Her worries seemed completely unnecessary if Michael's enthusiasm about the water park his father had taken him to was any indication!

Although the unlikely picture of the arrogantly aloof Alejandro Santiago in a public water park, full of tourists and children, took a little getting used to!

'Not what you expected?' He quirked dark, mocking brows in Brynne's direction as Michael skipped off happily to the kitchen to ask Maria for a biscuit and some fresh orange juice.

Not exactly, Brynne inwardly acknowledged as she hesitated about joining him at the table where he sat relaxing by the pool; after all, he hadn't wanted her company all day, so there was no reason to suppose that he would want it now, either.

Which was totally childish on her part, she instantly reproved herself impatiently. Whether Alejandro wanted her company or not, he was stuck with it for another three and a half weeks, and she had no intention of making herself scarce every time he was around!

'I'm sure the two of you had a wonderful time,' she said noncommittally as she pulled out one of the chairs to sit down, her legs aching slightly from the amount of walking she had done today.

Alejandro gave a slightly derisive smile. 'I enjoyed myself watching Miguel enjoy himself,' he drawled ruefully, his smile fading slightly as he added huskily, 'He is a charmingly engaging little boy.'

'Yes.' Brynne nodded. 'He is.'

'And that, I know, is due to the way Joanna and your brother brought him up,' Alejandro murmured softly. 'No doubt, your family too.'

'Oh, I don't think we can take too much credit for that,' she denied, a pleased flush to her cheeks nonetheless. 'Joanna had pretty much helped mould him into the happy, unspoilt little boy that he is by the time we all met him.'

'She was a good mother.' It was a statement, not a question, Alejandro knowing just from being with Miguel that this was so.

'The best,' Brynne confirmed unhesitantly. 'She seemed to find no difficulty at all in juggling her career as a very successful lawyer and her role as Migu—Michael's mother.'

Joanna had been twenty-four when Alejandro had met her, had completed her law qualifications and had been taking a year off from her studies to travel the world before commencing her career. It pleased him to know that she had had the success of that career that she had wanted so much.

He nodded. 'She was very determined, very positive, of what she wanted to do with her life.' There was sadness, if not actual grief, in his thoughts that all of that bright determination had been wiped out in a single act. 'I am glad she succeeded.'

'Yes,' Brynne said huskily, slightly uncomfortable with this conversation, in the circumstances.

'You find my interest in Joanna's life—strange?' Alejandro guessed astutely.

She shrugged. 'Well, yes, a little,' she acknowledged ruefully.

Alejandro shrugged broad shoulders, obviously relaxed from his day out with Michael, their own earlier tension seeming to have been put to one side, if not forgotten. 'She was the mother of my son. Of course I am interested in whether or not she was happy.'

'She and Tom were very happy together,' Brynne told him slightly defensively.

'I am aware of that too.' Alejandro gave an acknowledging nod. 'Miguel has talked of "Mummy" and "Daddy" for most of the day!'

Brynne became very still. 'He has?'

'Yes.' Alejandro gave her a quizzical look. 'This surprises you?'

Yes, it did. Apart from those nights when Michael woke up having nightmares, crying for his 'Mummy and Daddy', he never spoke of Joanna and Tom, hadn't openly cried for them, either. Brynne wasn't a psychologist, but she felt it was as if by not talking about them Michael could somehow put it from his mind that they were no longer there, that he could somehow believe they would one day walk back through the door.

The finality of death was very difficult for young children to understand, and only time and a great deal of love, Brynne knew, would help to heal the little boy's deep sense of bewilderment.

And having Alejandro Santiago as his real father…

Because, aged four when Joanna and Tom had married, Michael had obviously always known that Tom wasn't his father.

It was good that Michael felt he could talk to Alejandro about Joanna and Tom. Maybe Michael was already starting to transfer his affection to the other man…?

'I am a stranger, Brynne.' Alejandro broke the silence that had stretched between them. 'Perhaps he feels more comfortable talking of them with someone who he knows…and please do not misunderstand me, but I am someone that Michael knows will not become emotionally upset when he talks of his mother and Tom.'

That was a point.

It was also a point that Alejandro had for once forgotten to call him 'Miguel'…

She managed a rueful smile. 'You're probably right. I'm afraid my parents have been pretty well emotionally demolished by the whole thing, by Joanna's death of course, but Tom's especially. And I can't claim to have been too controlled about it myself.' She grimaced.

'But why should you be?' Alejandro frowned. 'Tom was your older brother, Joanna your sister-in-law. It was—is—a tragedy.'

Brynne gave him a quizzically searching glance. 'But without that tragedy you might never have known Michael was your son—'

'What sort of man do you take me for, Brynne?' he cut in frowningly. 'Do you think I would wish Joanna dead just so that I could claim Miguel?'

Well, she had pretty much put an end to that truce, Brynne guessed with a regretful wince for her inappropriate choice of words.

'Of course I didn't mean that,' she dismissed impatiently. 'I was just pointing out—'

'Brynne, I am very happy to know of Miguel's existence, and I hope that if Joanna had lived I would still have learnt of it one day when he had grown up and possibly asked about his real father.' He was consumed with anger. 'But I certainly do not feel any pleasure in the fact that his mother is dead!'

Brynne gasped breathlessly. 'You're deliberately misunderstanding me—'

'I do not think so!' Alejandro stood up abruptly, his face etched into hard, aristocratic lines. 'No matter what you may have claimed only days ago, Brynne, I am not the inhuman monster you believe me to be,' he bit out between clenched teeth before turning sharply on his heel and striding away.

He had thought Brynne had got to know him better than that in the last few days, felt deeply the knowledge that she still thought of him in that way.

Walking away seemed to be something Alejandro did a lot around her, Brynne acknowledged achingly as she watched him stride off towards the beach, bitterly dismayed at this fresh misunderstanding between them.

She turned sharply back to the villa as she heard the sound of glass breaking, knowing by the look of horror on Michael's white, shocked face as he stood a short distance away on the tiled patio, the broken glass of orange juice at his feet, that he had to have heard at least the tail-end of her exchange with Alejandro, if not all of it!

Brynne got noisily to her feet. 'Michael—' she didn't get any farther as the little boy turned on his heel—much as his father had done seconds ago!—and ran back inside the villa.

She hurried after him, all the time cursing herself for not remembering that as a teacher she was well aware of the fact that children had a way of appearing when you least expected them to—that, in Michael's case, his return hadn't been unexpected.

She should have realized, should have been more circumspect—

It was no good making the excuse that she had been so bemused by Alejandro's almost gentleness as he had spoken of Joanna that she hadn't given Michael's return a second thought—she should have thought!

Michael was her priority. And in this case she and Alejandro were responsible for causing him pain.

'Michael…!' She groaned as she found him in his room face down on the bed, quickly crossing the room to sit on the side of the bed and gather him up into her arms.

Michael clung to her, crying so hard his whole body was racked by the shuddering sobs. 'Mummy and Daddy are never coming back, are they?' he choked as he clung to her. 'I'm never going to see them again, am I?' he cried as he was besieged by fresh sobs.

Brynne was crying too by this time, the salty tears wetting her lips as she held Michael tightly against her.

'Are you going to die too, Aunty Bry?' Michael sobbed. 'And my new daddy?'

'No, Michael,' she gasped at his total desolation. 'Of course we aren't going to die.'

'Don't leave me, Aunty Bry!' Michael clung to her even harder. 'Please don't leave me!'

'Everyone dies one day, my love,' she added huskily, knowing that truth was very important to children; lose their trust once and it was very hard to regain it. And there were no guarantees when it came to life and death… 'But none of us is going to die yet, Michael. You'll be a man yourself, possibly with children of your own, by the time your new daddy or I die.' Surely fate couldn't deal this bereft little boy two such devastating blows…?

'That will be a long time then,' Michael breathed thankfully.

'Yes, a long time, darling,' Brynne confirmed huskily.

'Brynne…?'

She turned to look at Alejandro as he spoke softly to her from the doorway.

They made a desolate picture, Alejandro acknowledged even as he crossed the room to where they sat, both so emotionally wounded by this almost incomprehensible death of Joanna and Tom. 'I heard the breaking of glass and your shout of "Michael",' he explained huskily even as he sat down on the bed beside Brynne. 'I—'

'Daddy!' Michael had turned from his aunt's arms to launch himself into Alejandro's.

Alejandro felt emotion grip his own throat as he held Michael tightly to him, the little boy's arms clinging so pathetically about his neck.

'It is okay, Michael,' he soothed as he stroked that silky dark hair so like his own. 'Aunty Brynne and I will not leave you. You are not alone, Michael,' he assured him firmly. 'I promise you will never be alone.'

He was a man who chose to keep himself separate from

emotion, having decided long ago that it was better that way. But Michael's pain was such that it was impossible to remain unaffected. This was his son. His son! And Michael needed him in a way that no one else ever had.

He was filled with such a tidal wave of love that he found it almost impossible to speak, talking softly in Spanish when he finally found his voice again, reassuring his son of his love for him even as he stroked and held him close.

Not able to speak fluent Spanish, Brynne had no idea what Alejandro was murmuring to Michael, but it only needed one look at the softened arrogance of his face, and to hear the husky emotion in his voice, to know that it was something very personal, something totally private between father and son.

Feeling like an intruder on that emotion, she got quietly to her feet to walk over to the window. Michael had been so brave these last two months, so self-contained, that the release, when it had come, had been heart-shattering.

And when it had come, it had been Alejandro he had turned to for comfort...

She was glad.

For Michael's sake.

But mainly for Alejandro's.

He was a man who held himself so aloof from emotion, even knowing of Michael's existence, bringing him here, not seeming to have shaken Alejandro's well-ordered life too much. But she had seen love in Alejandro's eyes a few minutes ago, and knew that Michael's despair had finally broken through the barrier Alejandro seemed to have placed around his own heart.

Seeing Michael and Alejandro together like this, recognizing the affection, and now love, that was blossoming between the two of them, she could feel the trail of her own tears as they fell hotly down her cheeks.

'He has fallen asleep,' Alejandro murmured softly behind her a few minutes later. 'No doubt exhausted from the release of emotion,' he added huskily as he made his son comfortable on the bed before turning to look at Brynne. 'You and I need to talk,' he bit out grimly as he moved to the door, pointedly holding it open for her to precede him out of the room.

Brynne shot him a nervous glance as she reached his side, not at all sure of him in this mood, the tenderness he had shown towards Michael a few minutes ago having completely disappeared behind a hard mask.

Brynne swallowed hard. 'Perhaps one of us should stay with Michael—'

'You can come back and sit with him in a few minutes,' Alejandro assured her harshly. 'For now you and I have a conversation to finish. Not downstairs,' he instructed tautly as she moved in that direction. 'In here, where we cannot be overheard,' he added determinedly as he pushed open a door farther down the hallway.

'In here' was a room Brynne had never been in before, a huge, sunny room with double French doors leading out onto a large balcony, decorated in muted golds and browns, and dominated by a huge four-poster bed with gauzy drapes that could be pulled at night for complete privacy.

Alejandro's bedroom…

CHAPTER ELEVEN

ALEJANDRO saw the look of panic on Brynne's face as she realized he had brought her to his bedroom, his mouth twisting in derision. 'I am hardly in the mood for seduction at this moment!' He moved to the French doors, throwing them open to breathe in the clean, gentle breeze. He needed the fresh air to help him calm down. That scene with Michael had disturbed him.

'Michael overheard part of our conversation earlier,' Brynne told him unnecessarily.

They should have been more careful, of course, had once again allowed the antagonism that existed between them to spill out unchecked.

Brynne looked pale, her freckles once again standing out against the whiteness of her skin. Her darkly shadowed eyes showed that she was as disturbed by the incident as he was.

Unless finding herself in his bedroom had caused that…?

He gave an impatient shake of his head. 'The distress just caused to Michael has surely shown you that this habit you have of attacking me concerning my past relationship with Joanna has got to stop!'

Brynne gasped. 'You're blaming me—'

'We are both to blame,' Alejandro acknowledged harshly. 'You, for making accusations, judgements, you have no right to make. Me, because I felt the need to defend those judgements.' His eyes glinted angrily. 'My past relationship with Joanna is not your concern—'

'No, I just have to help pick up the pieces seven years later!' Brynne scorned, feeling stung by his words.

She accepted they had been wrong to argue like that in a place where Michael could overhear them. But she didn't accept the argument had been her fault. Alejandro was the one who had reacted to a perfectly innocent remark—

'Is that your only interest, Brynne?' Alejandro challenged, as he looked down his chiselled nose at her. 'Or is it that you feel some—personal curiosity, concerning my relationship with Joanna all those years ago?' he added softly.

Brynne felt the colour warm her cheeks. 'What are you implying now?'

His mouth twisted, there was o humor in his tone. 'There is a saying in your country, is there not, something about people in glass houses should not throw stones…?'

Brynne stared at him blankly for several long seconds, and then her eyes widened as his meaning became clear. 'If you're talking about what happened between us last night—'

'That is exactly what I am talking about, Brynne,' he sneered. 'How do you think that would have ended if we had not been interrupted in the way that we were?'

She had tortured herself with those very same thoughts alone in her bedroom last night…

'Is that why you did it, to prove—'

'We did it, Brynne,' Alejandro cut in harshly. 'I kissed you—certainly not to prove anything!—but once I had kissed you you were a willing participant to what happened next,' he reminded her coldly. 'So,' he clipped. 'What do you think would have happened?' he persisted.

'If your girlfriend hadn't arrived, you mean—'

'Oh, no,' Alejandro cut in softly. 'I am not going to allow you to antagonize me into changing the subject in that way.' He crossed the room to stand just in front of her.

Making Brynne all too aware of him, the heat of his body, that all-male smell, the leashed power that could be released at any second.

She avoided that compelling silver gaze as she moistened suddenly dry lips. 'I like to think—'

'No, Brynne!' Alejandro grasped her arms and shook her slightly. 'No thinking. No wishing. No imagining.' He shook her again. 'Tell me what you think would have happened after I had touched you here.' One of his hands moved to caress lightly across her breast before returning to grasp her arm. 'Kissed you here.' He held her gaze as his head lowered. His lips and tongue grazed lightly across her hardened nipple beneath her cotton top.

'Stop it!' Brynne struggled to pull away from him but was held tight by the strength of his hands on her arms.

'What if we had not stopped—for whatever reason—when we did, Brynne?' he repeated softly. 'What do you think would have happened next?'

She didn't need to think—she knew what would have happened!

She had wanted Alejandro last night, mindlessly, urgently. She had been unable to think of anything but him, of being even closer to him; she hadn't even been aware of the approaching car that had alerted him to Antonia Roig's arrival.

Alejandro could see the pained bewilderment in Brynne's eyes, could guess at the reason for it, knew that he was hurting her, but needed to make her understand the past.

It was this lack of understanding—perhaps of experience?—that caused her to judge him and Joanna as harshly as she did, and while he did not care for himself, Joanna was a different matter.

'We both know what was going to happen next.' He released her abruptly, moving several feet away to thrust his hands into his trouser pockets. 'The two of us would have become lovers—'

'No—'

'But yes, Brynne,' he insisted softly. 'We were almost there already.'

'You're despicable!' she gasped.

'I am honest,' he corrected grimly. 'With myself. And with other people. It is the same honesty that Joanna and I had between us seven years ago. We were not in love with each other, but we liked each other, were attracted to each other. It was an attraction that we acted upon. The same attraction that was between us last night—'

'No—'

'What are you saying, Brynne?' he taunted. 'That what you felt last night was not lust but something else? That you are in love with me?' he added derisively.

Of course she wasn't in love with him!

He was hateful. Arrogant. Mocking. And she despised him for discussing last night in this cold, analytical way.

That completely mindless passion had never happened to her before, with anyone, and it was something she still had trouble accepting, let alone understanding.

'Well, are you?' Alejandro continued remorselessly.

'No, of course not—'

'Of course not,' he echoed scornfully. 'But you allowed me to touch you, to caress you, to kiss you—'

'Stop it!' she cried emotionally. 'Just stop it!' She turned away, shaking.

'Yes, I will stop.' Alejandro sighed heavily. 'But you are a hypocrite, Brynne Sullivan. You are fooling only yourself by believing you are incapable of the same feelings that drew Joanna and I together seven years ago.'

Brynne knew she was fooling herself. She was totally aware of the fact that she wouldn't have been able to pull back from making love with Alejandro last night. She had wanted him completely. She had continued to ache for his possession for hours afterwards.

She still ached for that possession...

'You also blame me for the fact that Joanna went through her pregnancy alone, brought Michael up alone for the first four years of his life,' he continued determinedly. 'My defence to that is it was Joanna's choice—'

'Because you were married—'

'My marriage is immaterial. It was Joanna's choice not to tell me of the pregnancy or of Michael's existence,' Alejandro continued remorselessly. 'If anyone should be angry about that, then it should be me, not you,' he stated flatly. 'I am disappointed not to have known Michael until now, yes, but I do not blame Joanna for the choices she made. They were hers to make, after all.'

He was right. Brynne knew he was right. But it had been far easier to be angry with Alejandro, living, breathing, arrogant Alejandro, rather than Joanna, her feistily independent sister-in-law.

'I do not intend to discuss this subject with you again, Brynne,' Alejandro told her huskily. 'The past is gone. Joanna is gone. And so any further discussion on the subject is pointless. Harbour such thoughts as you want about me—I am sure that others have thought much worse,' he added dryly. 'But do not think those things of Joanna.' He sobered. 'She was a beautiful free spirit when I knew her, a woman who knew her own mind and body, and that is how I will always think of her.'

Joanna had been the same beautiful free spirit when Brynne had known her too, when Tom had fallen in love with her.

And that almost gentle way that Alejandro talked of her seemed to imply that his own emotions had not been as removed in that relationship as he would have liked them to be...

'There is only Michael now,' Alejandro continued briskly. 'He is all that is important.'

'I agree,' she said quietly.

'You do?' Alejandro sounded amused now.

She raised her head to look at him, that amusement also in his eyes. 'Yes, I do,' she confirmed ruefully. 'And I'll try not to be hypocritical again,' she added softly.

Alejandro studied her between narrowed lids, knowing exactly what she meant by that last remark.

Brynne intended to ensure that the opportunity to make love with her did not occur again.

He knew it was the sensible thing to do. The right thing to do. And yet sensibility was not an emotion this young woman aroused in him.

He had wanted her badly last night, had felt her quiver in response a few minutes ago when he had touched her, and knew he could not offer the guarantee, given similar circumstances, that it would not happen again…

'You will "try", Brynne…?' he taunted softly.

Her mouth tightened. 'Yes.'

Alejandro nodded. 'Then I will try also,' he murmured huskily.

'Although this is perhaps not the right room in which to make such an assertion?' He looked around them pointedly.

The sudden vision he had of Brynne lying naked with him on his four-poster bed, those golden limbs entangled with his, the fiery swathe of her hair cascading over his chest, was perhaps not conducive to such a claim either!

'I'll go back and sit with Michael now.' Brynne turned away from him abruptly.

'Brynne…?' Alejandro reached out to lightly grasp her arm. She stared up at him and he looked down into that beautiful but pale face; he saw the guarded emotions in those dark blue eyes.

Alejandro was overwhelmed with a desire to kiss her again, to touch her, caress her!

Instead he spoke harshly. 'I shall be out to dinner again this evening but I will speak to Michael before I leave.'

Brynne didn't need two guesses as to whom Alejandro would be having dinner with again this evening.

Obviously their discussion earlier had made no difference to his continuing a relationship with that other woman. No doubt Antonia Roig was sophisticated enough to deal with the sort of relationship Alejandro was used to, the only sort of relationship he would allow in his life.

The sort of relationship she and Alejandro had almost fallen into themselves last night…

Alejandro had been right to upbraid her on that subject. Her own response to him last night had made a complete nonsense of her assumptions about his casual relationship with Joanna all that time ago.

Last night she had been a victim of her own desire for this man. She knew even now that she could so easily have forgotten everything but Alejandro as his hands and lips had weaved a magic over her body that she had had no thought of denying.

Just the touch of his hand on her arm right now was once again weaving that magic…

'I'm sure Michael would like that,' she bit out.

'And you, Brynne?' Alejandro murmured throatily. 'What would you like?'

She would like him not to go to Antonia Roig! But to stay here with her this evening. For them to talk. To laugh. Before they made slow, leisurely love together.

Madness!

Her chin rose; she was determined to fight these feelings. And to go on fighting them.

'Once Michael is awake I would like to go and have a quick bath before our evening meal,' she dismissed lightly.

The thought of Brynne, those long, golden limbs completely naked, her hair secured loosely on top of her head as she floated in the Jacuzzi bath in the room that adjoined her bedroom, was almost Alejandro's undoing.

Instead he thrust her away from him, his expression harsh and remote. 'Go and bathe now, if you wish,' he rasped, forcing that image firmly from his thoughts. 'I will sit with Michael until you return.'

She looked at him quizzically. 'You've decided to call him Michael, after all…?'

'For the moment, yes.' Alejandro shrugged broad shoulders. 'Perhaps in wanting him to become immediately Spanish, I am expecting too much too soon.'

Brynne gave a rueful smile. 'I think that's very wise.'

'Wise, Brynne?' he echoed mockingly. 'I did not think you believed me capable of such an emotion.'

She believed him capable of many more emotions than she would care to admit, the main one, she realized as she continued to look up at him, being an integrity where the existence of his son was concerned.

Alejandro had remained in ignorance of Michael's existence for over six years, and even once he had seen the newspaper article on Joanna's death, and realized that her son could also be his own son, he could have continued to ignore that existence if he had chosen to. But instead he had claimed his son, had fought a legal battle with her in order to secure that claim. And through all of that he had maintained a respect and affection for Joanna that was unshakeable.

Alejandro Santiago, she acknowledged, was indeed an honourable man.

The fact that he resented her, and her earlier efforts to deny him his son, was perhaps the price she paid for that realization…

Her smile deepened. 'I'm sure that what I think of you is of absolutely no importance to you whatsoever, Alejandro!' she said with certainty.

Was it unimportant? Alejandro wondered. Last night he had made love with this woman, would have taken her completely if Antonia had not arrived so unexpectedly. How would Brynne have behaved towards him today if that had happened?

It would, he knew with sudden clarity, have made it impossible for them to continue to stay here together.

He gave a hard smile. 'None whatsoever,' he confirmed dismissively. 'Go and take your bath,' he instructed curtly before turning away, his back rigid, hands clenched at his sides as he stared out of the window until he heard the bedroom door close softly as Brynne left.

His breath left him in a shaky sigh as he forced the tension from his shoulders and slowly unclenched his fists.

This completely candid conversation with Brynne had been necessary and perhaps long overdue. Even though she didn't appreciate the comparisons he made between his past relationship with Joanna and what had happened between the two of them last night, it had needed to be said. Although it hadn't been deliberate, Brynne now knew that desire was as forceful an emotion as love was reputed to be.

Reputed. Because Alejandro had never loved any woman. Not Joanna. Not Francesca. Certainly none of the now nameless, faceless women he had been involved with over the years.

He wasn't in love with Brynne either, but nevertheless her flame-coloured hair, those candid blue eyes and that delectably arousing body had become a torment to him, a temptation.

It was a temptation he was finding it increasingly difficult to resist…

CHAPTER TWELVE

BRYNNE awoke drowsily as she felt herself being lifted, an arm about her shoulders, another beneath her bent knees. Her lids felt heavy as she looked up and found Alejandro's face only inches from her own, those two cradling arms obviously his.

'What are you doing?' she murmured sleepily.

He looked down at her, eyes dark and unfathomable. 'What does it look like I am doing?' he came back softly.

It looked—and felt—as if he were holding her against that muscled hardness of his chest. Brynne was able to hear the steady beat of his heart beneath the silk material of his shirt.

'I found you asleep on the sofa when I returned home,' he added huskily as he began to walk up the stairs.

Oh, yes, she remembered now. She and Michael had eaten a leisurely dinner together, her own meal accompanied by a couple of glasses of wine. After she had put Michael to bed she had sat in the sitting-room reading—still unable to banish thoughts of Alejandro out with the beautiful Antonia Roig—and must have fallen asleep.

She had been waiting for Alejandro to return, that was

it. She had something she needed to tell him. But cradled close against him like this she couldn't think straight, certainly couldn't remember what that something was!

'Where are you taking me?' She frowned.

Where indeed? Alejandro wondered as he looked down at her, the long red hair feeling like silk as it cascaded over his bare arm, her eyes once again that dark smoky blue, her face slightly flushed from sleep, those slightly parted lips so full and inviting.

It was an invitation, with her silk robe–covered body held so closely against him, the swell of her breast pressed to his chest, that he was fast losing the struggle to resist!

He had gone upstairs to check on Michael when he returned home shortly after eleven o'clock. He hadn't expected to find anyone still up, but the small lamp he had seen still on in the sitting-room when he had let himself in had drawn him back downstairs to investigate.

Finding Brynne there asleep on the sofa had been the last thing he had expected.

Or wanted, after earlier fighting the impulse he'd had to follow her to the bathroom and sit and watch her as she bathed.

She had sat curled up against the cushions, her beautiful face bare of make-up, the rumpled folds of her robe revealing the creamy swell of her breasts, those long, sensitive fingers, that had caressed his back so arousingly the night before, curled loosely about the book she must have been reading when she fell asleep.

Alejandro had looked down at her for several long minutes, drawn between the desire to lie down on the sofa beside her as he kissed and caressed her awake, and the more sensible idea of waking her so that she could get herself off to bed before he gave in to that desire.

In the end he had done neither, instead bending down to lift her easily into his arms with the idea of carrying her up the stairs to her bedroom.

She felt so light in his arms, so soft and silky, that he realized now he had been foolish to think he could simply carry her to her room and just leave her there. The rapidly rising desire in his body clamoured for him to do something quite different...

Brynne, fully awake now, looked up at Alejandro beneath lowered lashes, seeing his tightly clenched jaw, a nerve pulsing in one rigidly set cheek.

He smelt faintly of wine and expensive cigars, of a spicy aftershave, and underlying those scents was the all-male smell that was Alejandro.

And he felt wonderful, she discovered as her arms moved up about his neck and her hands rested lightly on those broad shoulders. He was warm and sensual to the touch, the heat from his body transmitting itself to her much cooler one—that heat seeming to increase as her fingers became entwined in the dark thickness of the hair at his nape.

He looked down at her beneath hooded lids. 'What are you doing, Brynne?' he rasped.

After their earlier conversation about the danger of the two of them being close like this, she wasn't quite sure, only she knew that she wanted to continue touching him. That she wanted more than to touch him. She wanted him to touch her too, to kiss her in the way he had the night before.

'Do not look at me in that way, Brynne,' he ordered, that nerve pulsing more rapidly in his cheek.

'What way is that, Alejandro?' she murmured huskily, slowly moistening her lips with the tip of her tongue, deliberately holding his gaze as she did so.

His mouth firmed impatiently. 'Have you been drinking?'

'Not as much as you have, I'm sure,' she dismissed, knowing it was Alejandro himself that was making her feel so wantonly reckless, not the two glasses of wine she had drunk hours ago and already slept off.

Alejandro came to a halt in the hallway as he looked down at her, knowing he should just take her to her bedroom and leave her there. But his own bedroom was nearer. And at this moment Brynne was so soft and willing in his arms…

His eyes narrowed. 'Are you going to regret this in the morning, Brynne?'

'Probably,' she whispered. 'But I'm trying not to be…hypocritical about it.'

His mouth curved into a smile at this joke directed towards herself.

'You are intoxicated—'

'With you,' she murmured throatily as she turned to where his shirt was unbuttoned, her lips lightly caressing. 'Only with you, Alejandro,' she assured him huskily before her tongue moved to taste him.

Dios Mío, he could perhaps fight his own desire, but he could not fight Brynne's as well.

He hesitated no longer, kicking his bedroom door open and then shut again behind them, before carrying

Brynne over to his bed, laying her down there amongst the cushions.

'I always wanted to sleep in a four-poster bed,' she told him huskily as he moved to release the drapes that enclosed them in their own private world.

Alejandro gave a rueful smile. 'Sleeping was not what I had in mind.'

Brynne returned that smile—if she was still asleep and dreaming, then this was a dream she never wanted to end!

Her arms moved up about his shoulders as she drew his head down towards her, her lips slightly parted as, with a throaty groan, he took fierce possession.

The last twenty-four hours since they had been together like this might never have happened, the desire between them instant, burning, out of control.

Alejandro's mouth continued to plunder hers as he pushed her robe and then her silky top to one side and bared her breasts to the caress of his hands. Brynne's back arched in invitation; she gasped low in her throat as she felt him first cup and then caress those swollen orbs, her nipples hard and sensitive to that touch.

Her hands moved restlessly across his back, nails slightly rasping through the thin material of his shirt, wanting to feel his skin in the way that he was caressing hers. Her fingers shook slightly as she unbuttoned his shirt and slipped it off his shoulders and down his arms.

Alejandro's mouth left hers reluctantly as he raised his head. 'Let me look at you.' He groaned, reaching out to switch on the bedside lamp.

She looked just as wild and wanton as he had imagined she would, her breasts small and perfect, the nipples a deep rose as he slowly lowered his head to suckle, first one and then the other. Drawing those hardened nubs into the moist heat of his mouth as he tasted and sucked, he felt the heat of Brynne's pleasure as her thighs began to move restlessly against him, asking for more, begging for more.

'I want to kiss and touch all of you.' Alejandro groaned as he placed a lingering kiss on each nipple before his hands trailed down across her ribcage to the slender curve of her hips, sliding down the silky material of her pyjama bottoms to reveal the silky auburn triangle between her legs. His hand moved to part and then caress her there.

Brynne had seen the beauty of her body in Alejandro's eyes as he had stripped that last remaining article of clothing from her body, her eyes widening slightly and then closing in ecstasy as he touched between her thighs. She moaned deep in her throat as she felt the touch of his lips against her now, gently seeking, and then finding, the tiny nub of arousal between her thighs. His tongue was a rasp and then a caress as she gasped in rising pleasure, his hand caressing before he entered her, matching that delicate thrust to the increasing caress of his tongue.

She hadn't known—hadn't realized—

And then she couldn't think any more as a pleasure unlike anything she had ever known before tore through her with the force of a tidal wave. Her body convulsed against his hand as he continued to lick that hardened nub until he had given her every last vestige of pleasure.

'So wet,' he murmured huskily as he continued to caress her. 'So hot and wet and ready for me.' He groaned hungrily, lips and tongue kissing and tasting as he moved slowly up her body.

Brynne felt as if she had been taken to heaven and back, had seen the moon and the stars, and Alejandro was the very centre of that universe.

She moved so that she could push him back against the pillows now, instinct taking over as she stripped trousers and boxer shorts from the lean strength of his body before bending down to taste him as he had tasted her, wanting, needing to give him the same pleasure.

Her tongue ran the hard length of him. Feeling empowered, she felt him spasm with pleasure, circling the tip of him before she took him into the moist heat of her mouth, her encircling fingers moving with the same gentle rhythm as her lips and tongue.

'*Dios mío*…!' Alejandro gasped in protest even as his hands reached out to become entangled in her hair and hold her tightly against him. His thighs moved to match those caressing hands and lips, the last twenty-four hours of damping down the release he had craved last night bringing him to the peak of release much quicker than he would have wanted.

'No, Brynne!' He reached down to stop her, lifting her up and on top of him before lowering her down again, the hardness of his shaft pulsing with his need to enter her tight wetness.

Brynne felt Alejandro's silken hardness move against her, reaching down to guide him into her, feeling a moment, a very brief moment, of pain, before he entered and filled her completely.

'You are so tight, Brynne,' he muttered achingly as his hands on her hips controlled her movements above him to the slow thrusts of his body. 'So erotically tight and perfect.' He groaned.

But she was so aroused, so ready for him, that the slickness of her body moved easily against his, taking them to even deeper heights.

'Beautiful, Brynne,' he murmured throatily, eyes dark as he gazed his fill of her breasts. 'You are so, so beautiful.'

She felt beautiful, totally feminine, the pleasure she was giving him, the pleasure they were giving each other, having taken away any shyness she might otherwise have felt at such intimacies.

Alejandro's hands moved up her ribcage to cup the pert swell of her breasts, his thumbs moving lightly across the sensitized tips. 'Let me kiss you again,' he groaned achingly even as he pulled her down to him and his mouth claimed her breast.

Brynne gasped, her hands on his shoulders, her head thrown back as Alejandro suckled the fiery tip of her breast into his mouth, the thrust of his hips against hers, the silken caress of his hardness, taking her to a climax that made her cry out in pleasure, her heat convulsing about him as Alejandro groaned and she felt him pumping his release deep inside her.

Seconds, minutes, hours later, she collapsed weakly down onto his chest, her rasping breathing matched by Alejandro's own as his arms closed about her and held her close against him, their bodies still joined.

'Next time we will go slower,' he promised gruffly. 'Next time I intend driving you to the point of madness before giving you the release you crave.'

Brynne felt so lethargic, so relaxed, so perfectly satiated, she couldn't even think past this moment, couldn't even imagine a next time.

Or could she? she marvelled as Alejandro began to slowly caress down the length of her spine before moving lower, his hands now cupping her bottom, fingers featherlight as he familiarized himself with every silken inch of her.

By next time, did he mean now? she wondered dazedly as she felt him begin to stir inside her. Surely it was too soon? Didn't a man have to rest for some hours before—?

'Ooh!' she gasped breathlessly as she felt his growing hardness against her sensitive inner flesh.

Alejandro grinned up at her wolfishly. 'I hope you are replete from your nap earlier, Brynne—because I really do not intend either of us to sleep tonight.'

Replete or not, Brynne could feel her own desire stirring, eager to know his body as intimately as he knew hers, wanting…

They both looked up as the telephone on the bedside table began to ring. Alejandro frowned. Brynne, in sudden panic, finally remembered exactly what the something was she had waited up to tell Alejandro!

'I forgot to tell you earlier,' she groaned in a rush of guilty apology. 'Your brother telephoned this evening while you were out—' She didn't get any further with her explanation as Alejandro disentangled their two bodies to lie beside her, frowning darkly before he turned to reach out and snatch the receiver from its cradle.

Alejandro's back was towards her as he took the call. He was speaking in Spanish so she had no idea what he was saying, but nonetheless Brynne was able to see the tension that stiffened his shoulders and spine as he listened to his brother's end of the conversation. It just made her feel even more guilty that she had forgotten to tell him of the earlier call. It had to be something important for the other man to have called Alejandro again at—at almost midnight, Brynne realized after a glance at the bedside clock.

How could she have forgotten to tell him? Brynne berated herself as she slid off the bed to push the drapes aside and pull on her robe. She was in the process of tying the belt securely about her waist as Alejandro ended the call, his face turned away from her as he stood up to begin pulling on his clothes.

'What is it?' Brynne frowned as she watched him.

Alejandro sat on the side of the bed to pull on his shoes, once again the arrogant Spaniard she had known for the previous six weeks.

'Alejandro…?' she prompted nervously.

'The chain of hotels we own in Australia are under threat of a takeover. I have to go,' he spoke flatly.

Brynne stared at him, unable to comprehend what he was saying. 'Go where?'

Alejandro shot her an impatient glance as he stood up. 'Australia, of course.'

He received a telephone call from his brother in the middle of the night, and he had to go to Australia?

What of their lovemaking just now?

Did that mean nothing to him at all?

CHAPTER THIRTEEN

BRYNNE stared at Alejandro incomprehensbly as he took a bag from the wardrobe and started to throw things inside it.

The two of them had been to bed together, had made love—wild, abandoned lovemaking on her part—and now Alejandro was just proposing to leave her as if it had never happened?

'Alejandro—'

'I do not have time for this right now, Brynne,' he cut in harshly as he finished packing his bag. 'I have to call my pilot and have him ready the plane for immediate departure.'

Her eyes widened as he picked up the telephone receiver and pressed several buttons. 'You're actually leaving right this minute?' Leaving her now, without any word being spoken between them about what had happened tonight...? 'That doesn't give me very long to wake Michael and pack our bags—'

Alejandro frowned as he turned to look at her. 'And why would you need to do either of those things?'

'So that we can come with you, of course,' she came back sharply.

Take Brynne and Michael to Australia with him after what had just happened? To have her there waiting for him at the hotel whenever he had a spare minute from the lengthy business meetings that would no doubt ensue once he joined his brother in Australia?

No!

He had no idea what had happened between himself and Brynne this evening. She had looked so appealing as she had lain on the sofa, and had felt so soft and warm in his arms as he had carried her up the stairs, that it had been impossible to do anything other than take her to his own bedroom and make love to her.

But Brynne, he knew, was not like the women he had been involved with since Francesca died.

For one thing she was the aunt of his son.

More importantly, he had become aware as they had pulled apart before he had answered Roberto's call—had seen the evidence himself on the sheet she had lain upon—that he had been Brynne's first lover!

He had never been any woman's first, had no experience whatsoever to draw upon to help him deal with that discovery.

His sudden departure might seem cruel to Brynne, but for himself Alejandro knew that he needed this time away from her, if only to consider where their relationship could possibly go after his discovery. If it went anywhere…

'Do not be ridiculous, Brynne.' Alejandro shook his head as he frowned down at her. 'I do not intend to take either you or Michael to Australia with me!'

'But—'

'Consuelo?' Alejandro said into the receiver as his call was finally answered, firing out instructions at a rapid pace before abruptly ending the call to turn and speak to Brynne once again.

Only to discover that she had gone…

Along with all trace of her, he noted with a frown, her pyjamas removed from the bedroom floor, only the rumpled bedclothes to show that he had not been alone in the bed a few minutes ago.

Alejandro drew in a ragged breath as he pushed back the dark swathe of his hair.

Going to bed with Brynne was not how he had envisaged his evening ending, and despite the excitement of their lovemaking he knew he had been less than gentle with her a few minutes ago, the discovery of her innocence having thrown his usually ordered life completely off balance.

For possibly the first time in his life he had not known what to do or say next, the urgency of Roberto's telephone call offering him an escape he had badly needed. Brynne's abrupt departure from his bedroom seemed to imply that she had needed to escape also.

He tidied his room slightly, removing those telling sheets, knowing Brynne would not care for Maria to know of the time she had spent in his bedroom.

Although he couldn't hide his frown when he got downstairs a few minutes later and found Brynne there in the hallway, fully dressed in denims and a body-hugging white top, her hair brushed and tied back from her face. He had not thought he would see her again before he left. In fact, he had hoped that he would not, felt that he needed time away from her to understand what had happened between them tonight before he even tried to discuss it with Brynne.

Brynne saw Alejandro's surprise—displeasure?—at

her presence downstairs, her heart sinking at the realization.

This was the man she had made love with such a short time ago.

The man with whom she had shared intimacies she had never known before with anyone, her body still aching in several places from the unaccustomed lovemaking.

The man who now seemed disinclined to talk about those intimacies.

Thank goodness.

Because one thing she was sure of, Alejandro regretted the lapse, and the worst thing she could think of was actually discussing what for her had been a wondrous time in his arms. For her their lovemaking had been unbelievable, so much more, so much better, than anything she might ever have imagined it could be.

That was due to Alejandro's experience, she knew.

It was that experience that made their encounter just another conquest for Alejandro. Tonight might have been something special to her, something undreamt of, but to Alejandro, if his urgency to get away from her was any indication—and she was sure that it was!—it obviously hadn't meant anything at all.

Sad, but true.

It was also true that a single business telephone call from his brother had been enough to change Alejandro from an ardent lover into the single-minded businessman she had always thought him to be…

The single-minded businessman she didn't doubt that he would always be.

He continued to frown as he drew in a harsh breath. 'I realize you think we need to talk, Brynne—'

'No, I don't think that at all, Alejandro,' she dismissed determinedly. 'In fact, I think the best thing for both of us is to forget tonight ever happened,' she added harshly.

Brynne wanted him to forget it. Alejandro scowled, his own earlier disquiet about the situation briefly forgotten. Forget the mind-blowing perfection of their lovemaking? Forget how beautiful she had been in his arms? Forget how her total arousal had sent him spiralling out of control?

He looked at her searchingly, but found himself unable to read any of her own emotions from her determinedly set features.

Forget it, she said. Would she be able to forget it? Would she just be able to put their lovemaking behind her when the time came for her to return to her life in England? Would she be able to forget him?

Despite his earlier confusion about their relationship, Alejandro found himself intensely displeased at the thought of that!

'And what if it is not possible to just forget it?' he rasped.

Brynne shot him a brief glance. 'I don't—' She broke off, her face seeming to pale as his meaning obviously became clear to her. 'There's absolutely no reason to suppose—'

'There is no reason not to suppose, either,' he snapped, her dismissal of any consequences from their lovemaking annoying him even further. 'Is there?' he pressed forcefully.

Brynne knew Alejandro had to be suggesting she might become pregnant from their completely unplanned lovemaking.

But surely the chances of that happening weren't that high?

After all—

'I obviously didn't use any contraception—did you?' Alejandro persisted with hard determination.

And Brynne wished that he wouldn't because she didn't need that worry to add to all the others she had. Such as how he now thought of her. More to the point, how she now felt about Alejandro!

Because if tonight had shown her anything, it was that any future for her without Alejandro in it—and she was pretty sure after this that he wasn't going to be!— was sure to be a bleak one.

'No,' she answered flatly. 'But that's still no reason to suppose there will be—any repercussions.' She frowned.

'Would you tell me if there were? Or would you be like Joanna and keep my child from me?'

Brynne winced at the bitterness behind the question. She didn't doubt that he respected the decision Joanna had made all those years ago concerning Michael's existence, but the harshness of his tone now implied that he felt angry with her at the same time. As he would be angry with Brynne if she were to do the same thing...

'I think that might be a little difficult, don't you?' she dismissed dryly. 'Michael will continue to be my nephew, a nephew I will expect to be able to visit in future, whether you like it or not,' she explained as she sensed Alejandro's waiting tension. 'I think, in the circumstances, I might find it a little difficult to hide the existence of a child from you!'

As an answer it was not very helpful, Alejandro acknowledged hardly. It certainly told him nothing of the emotions that had brought Brynne willingly into his bed in the first place. And he felt that he needed to know them in order to put what had happened between them tonight into its right perspective.

If there was a right perspective to what had happened between himself and Brynne!

Although Brynne's own reluctance to discuss what had happened seemed to imply that she had no answers, either...

'What will you tell Michael about my sudden departure?' he rasped.

It was a problem Brynne had been trying to find an answer to since the moment she had realized that Alejandro intended going to Australia on his own.

'The truth,' she snapped. 'That you've had to suddenly go away on business. I'm sure that it will be something that Michael will have to get used to in future!' she added disgustedly.

Alejandro sighed his impatience with her deliberate barb. 'Would you rather I didn't go, Brynne? That we continued where we left off?' he added scornfully.

Her cheeks burnt with colour. 'On the contrary,' she bit out hardly, 'I can't wait for you to go.'

His mouth thinned. 'Then on that we are at least agreed.'

'That has to be a first!' Brynne returned challengingly, determined, absolutely determined, that she was not going to break down in front of Alejandro.

That could come later, once she was alone. Alone with only the memories of their time together to haunt her. To taunt her.

Her mouth tightened. 'What do you want me to tell

Antonia if she should call at the villa or telephone?' she deliberately mocked him with the woman who should have shared his bed tonight.

'She will not,' Alejandro dismissed harshly.

'But she might.' Brynne grimaced just at the thought of having to deal with Antonia after the intimacies she and Alejandro had shared such a short time ago.

'Neither Antonia nor her father will call or telephone the villa, Brynne,' Alejandro assured her with such finality the statement couldn't be doubted.

Because, of course, Alejandro would call Antonia himself once he reached Australia, possibly even before that…

'Fine.' She nodded abruptly. 'You'd better go, then, hadn't you?' she added abruptly.

Brynne desperately needed Alejandro to go now, before the tears that threatened started falling down her cheeks and totally embarrassed her!

'Brynne…?' Alejandro's gaze was guardedly searching as he looked down at her.

'Oh, for goodness' sake, will you just go, Alejandro?' she snapped impatiently, her hands clenched so tightly she could feel her nails digging into her palms.

Because if he didn't soon leave she really was going to make a fool of herself!

Now that the time had come to leave her he did not want to go, Alejandro recognized frustratedly.

Which was ridiculous when minutes ago it was what he had wanted more than anything. To get away from her, and the memories of their lovemaking. To try, with many miles separating them, to make sense of what had happened tonight in regard to the relationship—that of father and aunt to Michael—they would have in future.

'Very well,' he bit out grimly. 'Maria knows my telephone number in Australia if you should need to contact me,' he paused to add huskily.

'I doubt the situation will arise,' Brynne dismissed without so much as a glance at him, her expression stony as she obviously couldn't wait for him to leave.

Alejandro gave her one last frowning glance before slamming out of the villa without so much as another glance in her direction, knowing that to do so could be his undoing, that to look at Brynne again, to remember their lovemaking, would result in him gathering her up in his arms and completely forgetting his resolve to put distance between the two of them until he could make sense of what had happened.

What was still happening, from the way his body had stirred with renewed desire when he was just looking at Brynne!

Brynne didn't move after Alejandro left.

Couldn't move.

Because with Alejandro's abrupt departure, she had made a mind-numbing realization.

She had fallen in love—desperately, completely, recklessly—with Alejandro Santiago…

CHAPTER FOURTEEN

'DADDY wants to talk to you, Aunty Bry!' Michael called excitedly even as she heard him running up the stairs to her bedroom.

Brynne straightened abruptly from where she had been packing a bag in readiness for them to go down onto the beach, intending to spend the morning there, already wearing a thigh-length blue cotton shirt over her bikini.

There had been many such telephone calls from Alejandro in the four days since he had flown to Australia so abruptly. One each morning, another each evening, his primary reason for calling to reassure Michael of course, although he always asked to speak to Brynne before ending the call. They were only stilted conversations on Brynne's part though, as she kept to telling Alejandro of the things Michael had done that day.

'Can you tell him I'm too busy at the moment to come to the telephone, please, Michael?' she dismissed lightly, shoving a towel into her bag as she did so, just knowing that Alejandro was on the telephone enough to rattle her nerves.

'Why not tell me that yourself…?' Alejandro spoke huskily from just behind her.

Brynne spun round with a gasp, her eyes wide as she looked at Alejandro standing so tall and powerful in her bedroom doorway.

The last four days had been difficult ones for her as she had tried to come to terms with the love she had realized she felt for this man.

The complete love that had drawn her to him, to his bed, four nights ago…!

But if those four days had been difficult ones for her, one look at the strain etched into that arrogantly assured face showed that—for totally different reasons, of course—they had been just as difficult for Alejandro.

Her heart was beating erratically, loudly, so much so that she felt Alejandro must hear it too. 'Why didn't you warn—er—tell us you were coming back today?' she said awkwardly as she put her hands behind her back so that he shouldn't see they were trembling slightly.

Alejandro's mouth tightened as he heard that correction in her question. Or rather—accusation… Because one look at Brynne's slightly defensive expression, the wariness in her deep blue eyes, was enough to tell him she was not pleased to see him again.

Which was a pity—more than a pity!—when he had wanted nothing else but to see her again the last four days!

He had known almost as soon as he had boarded the plane at Palma airport four days ago that he had made a mistake by leaving Brynne in the way that he had. But to have turned around and come back would have been a mistake too when he had still been uncertain of what he wanted from Brynne. Of what she wanted from him.

So he had flown to Australia as planned, where he and Roberto had dealt successfully with the attempted takeover. Once assured of that, Alejandro had wasted no time in returning to Majorca, needing to reassure Michael by his presence, of course, but personally needing to see Brynne even more.

A sentiment she obviously didn't reciprocate if her guarded expression was anything to go by!

His mouth twisted ruefully. 'It was a sudden decision.' He shrugged. 'I thought to surprise you.'

Oh, he had done that all right, Brynne acknowledged, still breathless from turning to find him standing in her bedroom doorway rather than on the end of the telephone line as she had thought him to be.

'I was surprised, Daddy,' Michael assured him as he beamed up at him, obviously pleased to see his father again.

Brynne was pleased to see Alejandro again, too—she just didn't quite know how she was supposed to behave towards him!

They had become lovers four days ago. But it was something that Alejandro had shown, by his abrupt departure, by his coldness towards her before he had left, that he regretted. She had no reason to suppose that these four days apart had changed that regret…

'Have you come back to stay?' she queried lightly. 'Or is this to be just a flying visit?'

His grey eyes glittered. 'Which would you like it to be?' Alejandro prompted softly.

Brynne felt herself tremble slightly as she recognized the expression of challenge in his eyes. Whichever way she answered that particular question was going to be wrong! If she said the latter, then it would look as if she didn't want him here. And if she said the former, then it made her look desperate for his company.

As Alejandro had been correct in his claim that she would not hear from Antonia Roig or her father while he was away, it had become obvious to Brynne that her assumption he would contact the other woman himself had also been the correct one...

She shrugged. 'I don't think what I want enters into it.'

He smiled without humour. 'Very diplomatic, Brynne,' he taunted. 'Michael tells me the two of you were on your way to the beach...?' He looked pointedly at the cotton shirt she wore over her bikini.

'Yes,' she confirmed huskily.

Alejandro nodded abruptly. 'If you wait five minutes I will come with you.'

'Oh, but—' She broke off her protest as Alejandro raised dark, mocking brows. 'Don't you have—calls to make and—and things you need to do, after being away so long?' she said awkwardly, knowing that the morning on the beach would be far from relaxed if she had to share it with Alejandro.

His mouth thinned. 'No,' he answered flatly, that grey gaze narrowed.

Brynne's heart was still pounding, her palms damp.

She simply had no idea how she was supposed to behave with the man who had become her lover. She didn't know the protocol and just found being with Alejandro again like this totally embarrassing. And the last thing she wanted was to be alone with Alejandro down on the beach, while Michael was snorkelling, and so give Alejandro the opportunity to actually bring up the subject of their time together four days ago…!

'Why don't just you and Michael go to the beach?' she suggested brightly. 'It will give you a chance to spend some time together, and I'm sure I can find plenty of things to do here.'

'Such as…?' Alejandro prompted softly.

Brynne frowned at him in frustration, knowing by his challenging expression that he was fully aware of her reluctance to spend time alone with him—and that he wasn't in any way going to help her to achieve that wish.

She grimaced. 'Well, I could—'

'Never mind, Brynne,' Alejandro rasped. 'Whatever they are I am sure they can wait.'

So was she—she just felt totally panicked at the thought of being with Alejandro again.

Alejandro had no idea what he had thought Brynne's reaction to seeing him again would be, but it certainly had not been this obvious wish to avoid even his company!

Especially when just being near her again like this was enough to tell him that all he wanted to do was take her back to his bed and make love with her once again. As he had ached to do the whole of the time he was away.

A feeling she obviously had not reciprocated!

'You would like Brynne to come to the beach too, would you not, Michael?' he prompted huskily—and then instantly felt guilty for using his son's affection for Brynne, and her affection for Michael—as Michael enthusiastically agreed that he would.

What did Brynne want him to do—beg for her company? Alejandro wondered frustratedly. Perhaps he might even be willing to do that if it would achieve the desired result…

'Then of course I'll come,' she agreed softly. 'I'll meet you both downstairs in five minutes,' she added dismissively, avoiding even looking at Alejandro as she turned to finish packing her bag.

Alejandro looked at her frustratedly. Wanting to shake her. Kiss her. Caress her. Anything that would bring a return of that warmly responsive woman of four nights ago.

Instead he turned abruptly on his heel and walked down the hallway to his own bedroom. Not that it offered any respite from these wild imaginings of Brynne, the four-poster bed a stark reminder of the time they had spent together there, his only consolation—if it could be called that—that Brynne did not seem to realize how deeply he regretted leaving her so suddenly that night. Brynne's own regret for what had happened between them was more than obvious by her lack of enthusiasm for his company.

Finding herself on the beach ten minutes later, Michael already off snorkelling in the shallow water, Alejandro lying on the sand beside her wearing only a pair of brief black swimming trunks that only added to the sheer male power he exuded, did not allay Brynne's feelings of panic in the slightest.

If just looking at him could send her pulse racing, and the heat coursing through her body, what chance did she have of spending the whole morning with him dressed—or, rather, undressed!—like this?

'You seem a little—distracted, this morning?' he prompted huskily as he picked up a handful of sand and watched as the grains fell softly through his fingers.

Distracted?

No, just totally aware of Alejandro...

She shrugged. 'I'm still a little surprised you didn't tell us you were returning, that's all.'

His mouth tightened. 'I told you on the telephone yesterday that the attempted takeover had been successfully blocked.'

Yes, he had, it just hadn't occurred to Brynne that success would mean Alejandro returning to Majorca quite as soon as this. She had thought she still had days before his return.

Not that it really made any difference when he returned—the first meeting between the two of them had been sure to be embarrassing whenever it was!

'You must be pleased that everything went so well,' she said noncommittally.

'Of course.' Alejandro gave an abrupt inclination of his head.

Brynne gave a tight smile. 'I expect you'll need to return to Spain to finalize everything?'

Alejandro's smile was no more humorous. 'You seem very anxious to get rid of me...?'

'Of course not—'

'Do not lie, Brynne,' he rasped coldly. 'You have made no effort to hide the displeasure you feel at my return.'

But that was only because—

Because she loved this man so much she actually ached with the emotion, her joy in seeing him again marred by the danger that he might realize how she felt about him!

Something she would find just too humiliating.

'Don't be silly, Alejandro,' she dismissed lightly.

'This is your villa, after all, and Michael is your son. You were bound to return some time,' she added practically.

'Your enthusiasm is overwhelming!' he drawled hardly.

Brynne turned away, breathing deeply. This was unbearable. This whole situation was unbearable.

'Brynne—'

'If you're going to talk about the other night—then please don't!' She turned to say shakily. 'I have no idea what happened—why it happened. It just did, okay!' she ended forcefully. 'And I really would prefer not to have a post-mortem on the subject!'

Alejandro looked at her searchingly. She looked so beautiful this morning, with her eyes sparkling, a blush to her cheeks and her mouth trembling slightly, that all he wanted to do was lay her down in the sand right now and make love with her.

Again and again...

She had been so responsive the other night, so shyly uninhibited, that he had found himself thinking of her often during the long hours he had sat in business meetings while in Australia.

From feeling irritated at having this woman foisted on him for a month, from not knowing four days ago what he wanted from their new relationship, he now knew that the thought of Brynne simply walking out of his life in a few weeks' time had become totally unacceptable to him!

'As of this morning,' she continued tightly, her gaze not quite meeting his, 'I can safely assure you there will be no unwanted repercussions, either!'

Unwanted?

He had pondered the question of Brynne being

pregnant with his child while he was away too. True, in Michael he already had one child who had been conceived out of marriage, and he would not willingly allow that to happen again. But if it had turned out that Brynne was pregnant it would have meant that she could not just walk out of his life…

'You must feel relieved,' he said softly.

'Of course,' Brynne dismissed lightly. 'As, I'm sure, are you,' she added derisively.

Was he? He was a man who usually had no doubts how he felt about anything, especially when it came to emotional complications, but Brynne Sullivan had slowly eroded all of that certainty over the last ten days, to the point that he was no longer sure of anything except that he wanted her!

'Of course,' he echoed, his mouth tight. 'Michael seems to have coped well since I've been away…?' He glanced over to where his son was now playing in a rock-pool.

Michael had coped with the separation from his father extremely well, Brynne agreed—she was the one who hadn't found it so easy!

Of course the memory of that time in Alejandro's bed wasn't exactly conducive to an easy mind—or emotions—but it was the realization of her love for this man that had caused her the most heartache.

How was she going to feel when she had to leave here? Had to leave Alejandro and Michael?

She nodded, also looking at Michael. 'We were talking about when you expect to return to Spain…?'

'You were talking of it,' he corrected harshly. 'But, yes, I think it is time that Michael was introduced to the rest of his family.'

Brynne swallowed hard. 'When do you expect to leave?' she prompted brittlely.

'Tomorrow,' he came back dismissively.

Tomorrow? So soon? Alejandro would be taking Michael and effectively flying out of her life tomorrow?

He shrugged. 'I have a few calls and business dealings to conclude, but I expect to have them completed by this evening, leaving us free to leave tomorrow morning.'

He certainly didn't intend wasting too much time here, did he?

Her mouth twisted ruefully. 'I'm sure that Miss Roig will be pleased to see you again this evening, even if you are leaving again so soon.'

Alejandro looked at her between narrowed lids. In any other woman he would have seen such a remark as possible jealousy, but in Brynne he saw it was merely a statement of fact.

He sighed. 'It is not my intention to see Antonia before I leave tomorrow.'

Brynne's eyes widened. 'It isn't...?'

'No,' he confirmed harshly, still angry with Antonia for having come here to the villa while he had been out and talking to Brynne in the way that she had.

'But—'

'Brynne, it has been obvious from the first that you have been under some sort of misapprehension where my relationship with Antonia Roig is concerned,' he bit out coldly. 'Considering our own—closeness, the other night, I find the continuance of such a misapprehension highly insulting!'

Brynne looked at him searchingly, remembering all the occasions when she had seen him with the other woman, the amount of time he had spent in the other woman's company, the fact that Antonia had come here and advised her to leave; what else was Brynne supposed to think but that the two of them were romantically involved?

Even though Alejandro had continuously denied such a relationship…

She gave a puzzled shake of her head. 'I'm sorry if I was mistaken—'

'Are you?' he scorned. 'I believe I have said this before, but it seems to me that you take some sort of delight in thinking the worst of me!'

There was no delight involved for Brynne at all in thinking of the woman Alejandro had married seven years ago, of his relationship with Joanna and the dozens of women he had probably been involved with since. Heartache better described her feelings where those women were concerned!

'You're talking nonsense, Alejandro—'

'I do not think so,' he bit out angrily, standing up. 'I will go and spend time with Michael—he, at least, expresses enjoyment in my company!' he added scornfully. 'We will not be returning to Majorca in the next few weeks, so you will need to take everything with you when we leave in the morning—'

'Excuse me?' Brynne cut in frowningly.

Alejandro scowled down at her. 'I am sure I made myself perfectly clear, Brynne,' he clipped impatiently. 'All of us will be flying to Spain in the morning.'

Brynne stared at him disbelievingly. He couldn't seriously expect her to go to his home in Spain with him—

But why couldn't he?

She had told Alejandro at the onset that she intended staying with Michael for this transitional month.

It had just never occurred to her that part of that month would be spent in Spain with Alejandro's family.

Or that by the time that happened she would have fallen in love with him…

CHAPTER FIFTEEN

BRYNNE swallowed hard, knowing it would be a wrench to be parted from Michael so soon, but also aware that she wouldn't feel comfortable being anywhere near Alejandro's family after what had happened between the two of them four days ago, and she wasn't comfortable being with Alejandro again…!

She drew in a deep breath. 'Perhaps when you take Michael with you tomorrow to meet your family would be as good a time as any for me to go back to England—'

'What are you saying, Brynne?' Alejandro cut in harshly.

She looked up at him with guarded eyes. 'That this might be a good time for me to go home—'

'You coward!' he rasped furiously, kneeling down on the sand beside Brynne to grasp her arms. 'How dare you just run away like this—?'

'I'm not the one who ran away!' she came back just as angrily, her pain still very raw. 'Perhaps you've also forgotten that my parents recently lost their only son? That they need me—'

'And perhaps you have forgotten that you agreed to stay with Michael for a month, not eight days,' Alejandro bit out coldly as he glared at her.

Eight days... Was that all it had been? Eight days, when the whole of her life had changed. When falling in love with this man had changed her for ever.

'You're hurting my arms, Alejandro,' she told him huskily.

Alejandro had thought of his abrupt departure four days ago not as the running away Brynne obviously thought it to be, but as a need to be away from her in order to make sense of his own emotions.

His mouth was a thin angry line as he thrust her away from him. 'You are a coward, Brynne—'

'That's the second time you've called me that,' she snapped angrily.

'Because that is what you are,' he said harshly as he glared at her in frustration. 'I do not believe for one moment that you are rushing back to England to be with your parents—'

'Well, I'm not rushing back to England to be with anyone else, either, if that's what you're implying!' Brynne breathed deeply.

It was not what he was implying. He knew Brynne well enough to realize that she would never have allowed their relationship to have developed in the way that it had if she had already been involved with someone in England.

Although she seemed to have had no trouble believing he could go to bed with her while still involved with Antonia Roig...

He stood up once again, aware that if he didn't do so

he might do something they would both regret. 'If you wish to go then you must do so, Brynne,' he told her flatly. 'But you need to tell Michael you are leaving him,' he added abruptly before turning away to stride over to the rock-pool where Michael was playing.

Brynne's eyes were so full of tears that she couldn't even see Alejandro as he walked away from her.

But she was doing the right thing, wasn't she? Putting as much distance between herself and Alejandro as she possibly could?

There was no future for them together. No anything for them together. So to stay, to go to Spain with them, to continue to be with Alejandro and continue to play the part of Michael's aunt, wouldn't help any of them.

Michael was comfortable with his father now, had talked of nothing else the last four days, and the two of them were chatting easily together as Brynne blinked away the tears to look across at them.

Only it seemed she was now uncomfortable being anywhere near Alejandro…

Because she loved him so much she ached with it, couldn't even look at him now without being afraid that love shone in her eyes.

Brynne was not leaving Michael, Alejandro knew even as he helped his son to collect shells, she was leaving him, could not even bear to be anywhere near him after what had happened.

Hadn't he retreated in the same way four nights ago? A decision he now was beginning to regret deeply, as he acknowledged an overwhelming need to keep Brynne beside him. He wanted to know that she would be there for him to talk to, to come home to, to make love to.

But four days of thinking of nothing but her and he had already known that he wanted all of those things with Brynne when he returned to the villa this morning.

And Brynne had made it perfectly clear that she wanted none of them with him.

That she was actually going to leave him tomorrow with the intention of never coming back…

How could he allow that to happen?

Did he have any choice?

'You have telephoned your parents…?'

Brynne looked across the terrace at Alejandro, her breath catching in her throat at how handsome he looked in the black evening suit and snowy white shirt, the darkness of his hair still damp from the shower he had taken before dinner.

A dinner she would much rather not have joined him for, but she'd known he would only call her a coward again if she attempted to excuse herself.

'Yes.' She strolled out onto the terrace to join him, cool and elegant in a fitted cream knee-length dress that showed off the tan she had acquired over the last few days.

Alejandro poured her a glass of white wine before looking up at her. 'They were pleased to hear of your imminent return?' he asked.

'I—didn't tell them,' she answered honestly as she sat down.

It was going to take months, possibly years, for her parents to accept Tom's and Joanna's death, but they had sounded much brighter when she had spoken to them on the telephone earlier, her father assuring her that her mother was off her medication now, and was even thinking of returning to work at the office where she had been a secretary for the last ten years.

It had been such a positive conversation, including her assurances about Michael's blossoming relationship with his father, that she simply hadn't got around to telling them she was returning home tomorrow.

At least, she had told herself that was what had happened.

In reality, she hadn't been able to commit herself to leaving once it had come down to it!

To leaving Alejandro…

Alejandro's gaze narrowed on her searchingly. She looked so cold and distant in her cream dress, her hair secured on top of her head adding to that elegant remoteness. Not at all like the love-tousled woman he had left so abruptly four nights ago!

He shrugged. 'Does that mean you have changed your mind?'

'I—no,' she said firmly before taking a sip of her wine. 'I don't know quite how to broach the subject with Michael, and I thought—I should talk to him about it before mentioning it to my parents.' She grimaced.

Alejandro gave a disgusted snort. 'It seems then that it is only with me that you are reticent!'

Brynne stiffened. 'I thought you would be pleased that I'm leaving—relieved, even—'

'I am not.' His accent was stronger in his anger, his eyes glittering dangerously. 'Brynne, you and I have became lovers—'

'Something that you clearly wanted to forget when you left so abruptly!' she cut in forcefully, colour warming her cheeks.

'But I have not forgotten!' He turned the full force of his attention on her as he sat stiffly in the chair. 'Neither, I believe, have you?' he rasped.

She closed her eyes briefly. 'I've—tried,' she said.

'But have not succeeded?' Alejandro prompted. 'Brynne, it is very important—' He broke off as the sound of a car could be heard coming down the long driveway to the villa. A scowl darkened his face at the possible interruption to this conversation.

Brynne had heard the car too now. And it didn't take two guesses to know who their visitor—who Alejandro's visitor!—was going to be. Obviously Antonia Roig had her own ideas about whether or not Alejandro would see her this evening.

She knew she had guessed the visitor's identity correctly as she heard the car engine switch off and the click of high heeled shoes on the pathway.

'It would seem that you have a visitor this evening,' Brynne murmured mockingly even as she heard Alejandro's muttered comments in Spanish as he slowly stood up, his face dark with anger.

He looked down at Brynne with glittering eyes. 'I assure you, she will not be staying,' he said harshly even as Antonia Roig appeared in the doorway behind a slightly frowning Maria.

Brynne stood up. 'I think I'll make myself scarce—'

'You will stay exactly where you are!' Alejandro's restraining hand on her arm reinforced his words even as he looked unsmilingly across at the beautiful Antonia Roig. 'What are you doing here, Antonia?' he clipped as the other woman strolled smilingly towards Alejandro with the obvious intention of kissing him.

Brynne felt a slight fluttering in her stomach at the coldness of his tone, knowing she would feel like cringing in a corner if Alejandro ever spoke to her like that.

Not that it seemed to deter Antonia Roig in the slightest as she continued to smile, sure of her own beauty and power in the figure-hugging red dress that showed off her olive complexion and her dark eyes. 'I would prefer for us to be alone, Alejandro,' she murmured huskily after giving Brynne a dismissive glance.

Alejandro's hand tightened on Brynne's arm as he felt her poised for flight. 'There is nothing that you have to say to me that Brynne cannot hear,' he assured Antonia, completely out of patience with this woman's machinations.

Antonia gave him a confident smile. 'I am sure that what the two of us have to say to each other can be of no interest to Miss Sullivan, Alejandro—'

'On the contrary,' he bit out scathingly. 'I feel it is very important that Brynne hear exactly what I have to say to you!' His mouth twisted derisively as he glanced at Brynne and saw how uncomfortable she was, those deep blue eyes pleading with him to let her leave.

It was a plea he could not grant. He had many things he wanted to say to Brynne tonight before she left tomorrow, and unwanted as Antonia's presence here was, it would help to dispense with one of those things!

He drew Brynne to his side before turning back to Antonia, those deep brown eyes hardening questioningly as she took in that show of intimacy. 'I have been engaged in a business transaction with your father, Antonia,' he said coldly. 'Nothing else,' he added grimly as she would have spoken. 'There has never been a relationship between the two of us. Nothing beyond a friendship extended to the daughter of a business acquaintance.'

Up to that point Brynne had been squirming with the need to absent herself from another display of the intimacy between Alejandro and Antonia, but Alejandro's apparent determination to establish that he had never been involved in any sort of intimate relationship with Antonia Roig made her stop squirming and look up at him searchingly.

Alejandro spared her a glance before turning back to the other woman, his expression becoming cold. 'But even my business dealings with Felipe were terminated, Antonia, after I learnt of your visit here to talk to Brynne when you knew I was away in Palma at a meeting with your father. A visit during which you took it upon yourself to tell Brynne she was not welcome here,' he added. 'English, Antonia,' he rasped as she began to answer him in Spanish. 'I want Brynne to know exactly what we say to each other.'

'Did she tell you I said that?' Antonia asked, giving a dismissive laugh and shooting Brynne a contemptuous glance. 'Alejandro, I can assure you that—'

'There is no necessity for you to assure me of anything, Antonia,' he replied coldly. 'I had to choose which one of you to believe, and I chose Brynne—'

'She has bewitched you!' Antonia said scornfully, her gaze hardening even more as she turned to glare at Brynne furiously. 'Into her bed, no doubt—'

'You go too far, Antonia!' Alejandro rasped icily.

'Only because I am—concerned, for you, Alejandro.' Antonia's voice softened huskily as she looked up at him. 'I merely suggested to Miss Sullivan that day that she might want to leave, that she is not of our type—'

'I thank God that she is not of your type,' he bit out scathingly. 'You will leave now, Antonia,' he added coldly. 'You will not come here again. You will most certainly never speak to Brynne again in the way that you did.'

Brynne felt a shiver down her spine at the cold anger in Alejandro's voice, knowing by the way Antonia Roig had paled that she was as aware of the implacability of his tone as Brynne was.

But there was only a momentary pause and then Antonia Roig's chin rose challengingly, her expression arrogantly contemptuous as she looked at them both. 'You are a fool, Alejandro,' she told him sneeringly. 'With my father's business connections, and the money I will eventually inherit as his only child, you and I could have been a formidable pair. And instead you choose to consort with this—this—'

'Careful, Antonia,' Alejandro warned softly. 'You are talking of a woman I hold in high regard, a woman of integrity and honesty. Attributes that are obviously completely alien to you!' he added coldly.

Brynne could only stare up at Alejandro in wonder as, after one last sneering glance in Brynne's direction, the other woman turned on her heel and walked briskly away.

Alejandro held her in high regard…? Believed her to be a woman of integrity and honesty…?

Even more confusing, why had he felt a need to make her a witness to all of those things he said to Antonia Roig…?

CHAPTER SIXTEEN

BRYNNE continued to watch Alejandro as he started to pace the terrace, his expression making her hesitate to ask any of the things that hovered on the tip of her tongue.

What if Alejandro had just wanted her to know that, as Michael's father, he was the man of honour he had always claimed to be? That his motives for making her a witness to that conversation with Antonia Roig were that simple? What if—?

'What are you thinking now, Brynne?' Alejandro paused to look at her, his tone rueful. 'Do you still remain unconvinced as to the innocence of my relationship with Antonia?'

Brynne shook her head. 'What I am puzzled about is why you think I needed to hear that…?'

Alejandro looked at her searchingly, wanting to see some sign in her demeanour that his lack of any intimate relationship with Antonia actually meant something to Brynne. But he could read nothing from her expression except that mild curiosity.

But he had gone too far now, was too aware of the danger of Brynne leaving to go back to England tomorrow, to draw back from the decision he had made earlier as he had sat on the terrace waiting for Brynne to join him. He could not let her go without at least telling her something of how he felt. What happened after he had done that was completely up to Brynne.

He was a man used to making decisions, and then acting on them, and it was not a pleasant position to find himself in…

He drew in a ragged breath. 'We need to go back to the beginning again for me to be able to explain that. To my relationship with Joanna,' he said as Brynne continued to look puzzled.

She stiffened. 'Haven't we already discussed that enough—?'

'No!' Alejandro rasped. 'The relationship, yes. Joanna's feelings about that relationship, also yes. But my own motivation behind the relationship? The reason that I was married to another woman only three months after that relationship? No.' He shook his head, his expression grim. 'I do not think we have discussed those at all.'

No, they hadn't—and Brynne wasn't sure she wanted to hear them now, either. Besides, what possible bearing could they have on the here and now…?

Alejandro gave a humourless smile. 'You would prefer to continue thinking of me as a man who uses and discards women, I think,' he muttered huskily.

She felt the warmth in her cheeks. 'I have never said that.'

'Your face has said that,' he assured her dryly.

'The fact that you also believe that I intend to discard you in that way also says that,' he added grimly.

Brynne swallowed hard as she saw his concerned

expression. A concern that he quickly masked as that arrogant pride fell into place once more.

He continued. 'As you have no doubt guessed, I was already engaged to Francesca when Joanna and I met seven years ago. It was an arranged marriage, not a love match. Our parents had decided on it while we were still children. It was to be the marriage of two powerful, rich families rather than Francesca and I.' He shook his head. 'I met Joanna in Australia, at a time when I was trying to decide how best to extricate myself from a situation, an engagement, I no longer wanted.'

'Alejandro—'

'You will do me the courtesy of letting me tell you these things, Brynne!' he rasped. 'You will have plenty of opportunity when I have finished to criticize and chastise!' he added derisively.

What he had already told her was enough to make her revise some of the opinions she had formed before accompanying him and Michael to Majorca.

'Joanna knew of my engagement to Francesca. She and I—talked about it. Joanna could not even begin to imagine marrying someone she did not love. As no longer could I.' He sighed. 'Joanna and I were not in love with each other, either, but she helped me to understand that I had to talk to Francesca, to see if she would release me from the engagement. But before I could do so I received an urgent call from Spain. My father had had a heart attack. To even contemplate causing such a scandal when he was so seriously ill was unthinkable. Can you understand that' he asked.

Of course she could understand. She knew how binding these arranged engagements could be, that they were usually arranged for the advancement of the family rather than the individuals who ended up married to each other.

'You married Francesca knowing that the two of you didn't love each other.' She nodded. 'I—have to agree with Joanna, I can't imagine anything worse!'

He nodded abruptly. 'It was an unhappy marriage from the first. We both tried—Francesca wanted to be a dutiful daughter, you understand?'

'As you wanted to be a dutiful son,' Brynne acknowledged, unable to stop the slight anger she felt towards the parents who had forced them into such a marriage.

'As I wanted to be a dutiful son.' Alejandro gave an inclination of his head. 'As I tried to be a dutiful husband. Whether you believe it or not, Brynne, I was a faithful husband,' he added.

She grimaced. 'Why shouldn't I believe you, Alejandro?'

'Many reasons,' he sighed. 'I was unfaithful during my engagement when I had my brief relationship with Joanna. I have had many relationships since my marriage ended.'

He wasn't going to spare himself—or her!—any of the hurtful details, was he? Brynne acknowledged ruefully. Although the fact that he was telling her at all, when she knew he wasn't a man who ever opened up about himself, was starting to make her wonder if there wasn't some purpose behind the explanation…

'Unfortunately, Francesca was not a dutiful wife.' He gave a slight shrug. 'Who could blame her? Nineteen years of age, and married to a man she did not even know, let alone love! Within a year of our marriage she had taken a lover. It is not so unusual in such marriages, although it is normal to wait until after the first son is born,' he added. 'To ensure that the husband knows that at least the heir is his!'

'What happened to Francesca, Alejandro?' she prompted huskily.

He looked grim. 'She died while giving birth to her lover's child. The child died, too.'

Brynne gave a pained gasp.

'Are you not going to ask me how I knew the child belonged to her lover?' Alejandro looked down at her.

A pose Brynne was now beginning to realize was as much a defence as anything else. Alejandro might not have loved his wife, but now that Brynne had come to know him better she didn't doubt that once married to Francesca he would have honoured the marriage.

She gave him an encouraging smile. 'Because you weren't her lover…?'

Alejandro felt some of the tension leave him, realizing as he did so just how tense he actually was. But this was important to him. That Brynne believed him was important to him. Much more important than anything else ever had been…

'Because I was not her lover,' he echoed. 'We were lovers—if it can be called that—for only the first three months of our marriage. I do not believe it was something that either of us particularly enjoyed,' he said ruefully, remembering those months when they'd tried to force a feeling of love for each other, an emotion that had never happened. 'Whereas making love with you four nights ago—'

'Alejandro—'

'I was wrong to leave you in the way that I did,' he told her forcefully. 'My only excuse—and it is perhaps not an acceptable one—is that I thought it for the best. I did not understand what was happening between us. But these four days away from you— I have thought of nothing but you, of our time together. Would you like to know why, Brynne?'

Brynne looked at him questioningly, not sure yet what he wanted from her. But she had no doubts that he was being honest; didn't she at least owe him the same?

'Yes,' she answered huskily. 'Yes, Alejandro, I want to know why you have thought of me the last four days.'

'Because our time together was beautiful,' he told her gruffly. 'Making love with you was more beautiful than anything else I have ever experienced.'

Brynne felt a lump form in her throat, hot tears clouding her vision. Because making love with Alejandro had been beautiful for her too.

Alejandro moved to clasp her hands in his as he looked down at her intently. 'It stunned me to learn of your inexperience.' He put up a hand to smooth her hair back from her face as he looked down at her. 'Beautiful, beautiful lovemaking,' he groaned huskily. 'I swore after my disastrous marriage that I would never become involved in that way with anyone ever again. But having got to know you— I am not proud of the way I behaved when I left you so abruptly. My only excuse is that I feared what you made me feel. But please believe me, Brynne, when I tell you I have thought of nothing else but you these last four days, of being in your arms again,' he admitted.

She looked up at him. 'I thought—you seemed so—angry, before you left…?'

He shook his head. 'Not anger, Brynne. Never anger. You had given me a precious gift that night, and I— ungracious swine that I am—did not know how to accept it!'

Brynne hadn't thought of it as a gift at the time, had only wanted to be with Alejandro. To be with the man she loved.

Alejandro's arms tightened about her. 'Brynne, I do not want you to leave me tomorrow.'

Her breath caught in her throat as she looked up at him, at the emotion in those softened dove-grey eyes, an emotion she thought she recognized, but found incredible in this man.

'I suppose I could come with you and Michael to Spain for a couple of weeks—'

'That is not what I mean, Brynne.' His voice hardened. 'I—even now this is difficult for me!' He released her to move away, running a hand through the dark thickness of his hair. 'Try to understand, Brynne, I have never been in love with anyone, was determined that I never would be after my marriage was so painfully unsuccessful—'

'I haven't asked you for love, Alejandro—'

'You do not need to ask!' He turned to her. 'Because the last four days away from you have shown me that I do love you, Brynne. More than life itself. More than anything and anyone,' he said shakily. 'The thought of you leaving me tomorrow, of you ever leaving me, is not something I can even contemplate!'

Brynne stared at him, at the assured, aloof man that she loved with all her heart, at the man who was no longer aloof at all, let alone assured.

Warmth began to course through her, to wipe away all the dread she had felt at the thought of parting from him.

Alejandro loved her.

Alejandro Miguel Diego Santiago loved her.

After the way he had left her four days ago she had never thought—had never even begun to hope—that he could return the feelings she had for him, hadn't understood at the time that what she had seen as his desertion he had seen as a sense of self-protection.

Only to come back today and tell her that he did love her. More than anything or anyone. Challengingly. Defensively. As if he feared the pain she could inflict on him if she chose to do so.

She moved to stand in front of him, their bodies almost touching as she looked up into his face. 'I love you too, Alejandro,' she breathed huskily. 'I love you so much that the thought of leaving you has been impossible for me to contemplate, either—' She got no further as Alejandro swept her up into his arms, her body held against the hardness of his as his mouth claimed and captured hers in a kiss full of the hunger he had felt for the four days of their parting.

It was a need Brynne felt too, holding nothing back as she returned the heat of his kiss, her arms up over his shoulders as her fingers became entangled in the dark thickness of his hair.

Alejandro wanted to devour her, to have her take him so deep inside her body that it would be impossible to tell where Brynne ended and he began.

Brynne was his flame. White-hot. Burning. That heat cleaving him to her side for all time.

He was breathing deeply when at last he raised his

head to look down into her flushed face. 'You do love me…' he said in wonder, knowing that it was true, that his honest Brynne could never be anything but truthful with him, in her emotions as well as her words.

She smiled up at him. 'Of course I love you, Alejandro.' Her fingers moved lightly down the clenched line of his jaw. 'You are everything—everything I could ever want in the man I love. You're a wonderful son. An affectionate and caring father. A man of honour in all things, including your relationships—'

'And you, Brynne?' he cut in searchingly. 'What am I to you, Brynne?'

'That's easy.' She smiled tremulously. 'You're the man I will love all my life.'

His breath caught in his throat at the simple statement that meant everything to him.

He had decided long ago that love and marriage were not for him, that Francesca had married him but had not loved him. The women he had known before her and since her had taken him, and all the things he could give them, but had not given him love.

Brynne gave him love, all her love, without asking for anything in return except that he love her too.

And he wanted to give her so much more than that! Everything that he was. Everything that he would be.

'Will you marry me, Brynne?' he prompted huskily, his arms tightening about her instinctively as she stiffened to look up at him dazedly. 'What did you think, *querida*? That I would tell you I love you, would listen while you tell me you feel the same way, and that I would then dishonour such a love with less than I offered to a woman who did not love me as I did not love her?'

She shook her head. 'I didn't think anything. I never thought, never dreamt, that you would ever love me…'

He frowned darkly. 'If I had never known you, Brynne, I would never have known what it is to love and be loved. Do you honestly think I could ever let such a love escape me by offering you less than marriage, less than everything that I am, that I have to give?'

Brynne hadn't known what to expect after admitting that she returned the love Alejandro told her he felt for her. Perhaps a brief relationship, a brief, beautiful relationship that would have to sustain her for the rest of her life. Marriage was something that she had never dreamt Alejandro would ever offer to any woman again…

She swallowed hard. 'But marriage, Alejandro.' She shook her head. 'You told me you would never marry again.'

'To a woman who did not love me, no!' Alejandro assured her with some of his old arrogance, his arms like steel bands about her. 'But you are different, Brynne. In the short time I have known you you have become the air I breathe, the perfume that warms my pillow, the very essence of my life. I will allow nothing, and no one, to come between us ever again.'

He was talking of Antonia Roig, and other women like her, women who only wanted to take and to use him, not to love him as he so deserved to be loved. As Brynne loved him…

'If you do not agree to marry me for love then I will have to try to tempt you into a marriage with me for Michael's sake.' He raised his eyebrows as he looked down at her.

But Brynne could see the humour lurking in his grey

eyes, the self-derision mixed with a determination that told her he would resort to such methods if all else failed.

'A marriage of convenience, you mean?' she drawled teasingly.

'A marriage that will give me the right to hold you, to love you, to come to your bed every night for the rest of our lives!' he corrected softly.

'Oh, no, Alejandro—'

'Oh, yes, Brynne,' he said firmly.

She shook her head. 'It will give us both the right to hold each other, to love each other, to come to our bed every night for the rest of our lives,' she corrected pointedly. 'If I have one condition to marrying you, Alejandro, then it's that we have a huge four-poster bed to share wherever we might be!'

He tilted his head teasingly. 'That is your only condition…?'

She laughed huskily. 'No conditions, Alejandro!' she assured him happily. 'I would marry you, will always love you, even if I have to live in a shack on the edge of a beach for the rest of my life!' She threw her arms about his neck. 'I love you, Alejandro Miguel Diego Santiago! I love you. I love you!'

Alejandro gathered her even closer into his arms, moulding her against him, knowing her to be the other half of him, the woman who completed him, who made him whole. 'I will love you for our lifetime and beyond, Brynne,' he whispered.

'As I will love you, Alejandro,' she vowed.

'Juanna Mercedes Santiago and Roberta Magdalena Santiago,' Brynne murmured emotionally as she looked up from gazing down at her newly born daughters into the face of the man she loved beyond words or expression.

Alejandro.

Her husband. Her lover. Her best friend. And now, almost a year to the day after their marriage, the father of their twin daughters.

Alejandro fiercely returned that gaze. 'They are truly beautiful, Brynne, but not as beautiful, or courageous, as their mother!' He shook his head. 'I could not bear to see you suffer so ever again!'

Brynne laughed. 'Childbirth isn't suffering, my love,' she assured softly.

A year of marriage had given them a bond of love so deep that it could never, ever be broken, only added to. As the birth of their daughters had done. They had become Michael's parents too, and had been absorbed into Alejandro's loving family as he had been accepted into her own family. They had delighted in each new discovery about each other.

Brynne reached up and touched her husband's cheek, smoothing away the worry and strain he had suffered as he had held her hand through the hours of childbirth. 'I love you, Alejandro,' she told him earnestly. 'Enough and more to have half a dozen babies—'

'Half a dozen!' Alejandro cut in forcefully, his expression only relaxing as he saw how she was teasing him, this beautiful woman he loved to distraction. 'Maybe two more,' he countered.

Brynne laughed softly. 'Maybe three…?'

Maybe three, he conceded achingly, knowing there was nothing he could deny this woman who meant more to him than life itself.

His wife.

The mother of his children. All his children. However many they might have.

The woman who loved him more than he had ever thought it possible to be loved.

But most of all, the woman that he would love, fiercely, passionately, beyond life itself...

* * * * *

Harlequin is 60 years old,
and Harlequin Blaze is celebrating!
After all, a lot can happen in 60 years,
or 60 minutes…or 60 seconds!
Find out what's going down in Blaze's
heart-stopping new mini-series,
FROM 0 TO 60!
Getting from "Hello" to "How was it?"
can happen fast….

Here's a sneak peek of the first book,
A LONG HARD RIDE
by Alison Kent
Available March 2009

"Is that for me?" Trey asked.

Cardin Worth cocked her head to the side and considered how much better the day already seemed. "Good morning to you, too."

When she didn't hold out the second cup of coffee for him to take, he came closer. She sipped from her heavy white mug, hiding her grin and her giddy rush of nerves behind it.

But when he stopped in front of her, she made the mistake of lowering her gaze from his face to the exposed strip of his chest. It was either give him his cup of coffee or bury her nose against him and breathe in. She remembered so clearly how he smelled. How he tasted.

She gave him his coffee.

After taking a quick gulp, he smiled and said, "Good morning, Cardin. I hope the floor wasn't too hard for you."

The hardness of the floor hadn't been the problem. She shook her head. "Are you kidding? I slept like a baby, swaddled in my sleeping bag."

"In my sleeping bag, you mean."

If he wanted to get technical, yeah. "Thanks for the

loaner. It made sleeping on the floor almost bearable."
As had the warmth of his spooned body, she thought,
then quickly changed the subject. "I saw you have a loaf
of bread and some eggs. Would you like me to cook
breakfast?"

He lowered his coffee mug slowly, his gaze as warm
as the sun on her shoulders, as the ceramic heating her
hands. "I didn't bring you out here to wait on me."

"You didn't bring me out here at all. I volunteered to
come."

"To help me get ready for the race. Not to serve me."

"It's just breakfast, Trey. And coffee." Even if last
night it had been more. Even if the way he was looking
at her made her want to climb back into that sleeping
bag. "I work much better when my stomach's not
growling. I thought it might be the same for you."

"It is, but I'll cook. You made the coffee."

"That's because I can't work at all without caffeine."

"If I'd known that, I would've put on a pot as soon I
got up."

"What time *did* you get up?" Judging by the sun's
position, she swore it couldn't be any later than seven
now. And, yeah, they'd agreed to start working at six.

"Maybe four?" he guessed, giving her a lazy smile.

"But it was almost two..." She let the sentence
dangle, finishing the thought privately. She was quite
sure he knew exactly what time they'd finally fallen
asleep after he'd made love to her.

The question facing her now was where did this relationship—if you could even call it *that*—go from here?

* * * * *

*Cardin and Trey are about to find out that
great sex is only the beginning....
Don't miss the fireworks!
Get ready for
A LONG HARD RIDE
by Alison Kent
Available March 2009,
wherever Blaze books are sold.*

EXTRA

THE BILLIONAIRE'S CONVENIENT WIFE

Forced to the altar for a marriage of convenience!

He's superrich, broodingly handsome and needs a bride in name only....

She's innocent yet defiant, and she's about to be promoted from mistress to convenient wife!

Look for all of our exciting books in March:

www.eHarlequin.com

HPE0309